# Serenity's Child

CONTENT WARNING: This book contains sexually explicit scenes and language that may be considered offensive to some readers. It is intended for purchase by ADULTS ONLY, as defined by the laws of the country in which the purchase was made. Every precaution should be taken to ensure that underage readers are not allowed access.

Wordsmiths, Ink LLC

Published by Wordsmiths, Ink, Gilbert, AZ

This is a work of fiction. Names, characters, places, and incidents are the product of the author's imagination and have been used to create this work of art. Any similarities to actual persons, living or dead, events, etc. is completely coincidental.



Paperback ISBN: 979-8-9995029-6-4

eBook ISBN: 978-1941142837

# Serenity's Child

**SHELBY KENT-STEWART**

Chase your dreams but
always know the road
that'll lead you home again.
**Tim McGraw**

# Chapter 1

"Hmm. Yummy."

Focused on plucking the bacon from her Cobb Salad, Sabrina Shelton wrinkled her nose. "Carly, I've been back two weeks and every day we meet at the same café and you order the same disgusting thing. There's no way a grilled cheese and banana sandwich can be yummy."

"Says you. Since when did you become a foodie? If I recall correctly, you like to eat worms. And why the heck don't you just order the damn salad without bacon?"

"I think pregnant lady needs a nap." Bri grinned as a wave of nostalgia doused her in warmth, the silly chit-chat, the sounds and smells of home. Like old times. Better times. "I was five when I ate the worm, and if you weren't on a constant hormonal high, you'd have noticed I always order the salad without bacon. Apparently a meal isn't a meal in Texas unless it includes the remains of a dead animal, which should probably be the state motto."

"Point taken but I wasn't talking about my sandwich. I was referring to him."

Following her friend's nod to the plate glass window, Bri felt a flutter in her tummy. Across the street and deep in conversation with Carly's brother was the personification of yummy. Well over six-feet with skin like burnished copper, he had a body beyond drool-worthy, muscled and toned, but it was his face that made her heart race. Framed by raven black hair that kissed his shoulders, it was chiseled and intense, the face of a warrior who would kick ass and not bother taking names. "Who is he?"

"Jace Malone, half-Sioux, half white, and one hundred percent delicious."

The name was familiar, but for the life of her Bri couldn't place it. "I give up. Who's Jace Malone?"

"Come to think of it, you two probably just missed one another, although how that's possible amazes me. Serenity's a burg. Everyone knows everyone."

A burg was putting it mildly, more like a gravel pit with amenities, and not too darn many of those. "You seem to forget I haven't lived here my whole life. After granddad sent me to school back East, I was only here during the summers. Aside from hanging out with you and your family, I never really assimilated back into the community. Then when I started college…" She shrugged. "The rest is history."

"The rest is scary, Bri. After what happened in Afghanistan, how can you even think about going to Syria?"

Good question. Afghanistan changed everything. After months of refusing assignments and cloistering herself in her Boston apartment, of licking her wounds and trying to make sense of the senseless, she was still off her game. Syria would be the ideal venue to work through her fear, assuming she lived through it. "You haven't told anyone about Afghanistan, have you, Carly? The people here already look at me with contempt. I don't need their pity."

"I haven't even told Tommy and I won't breathe a word, but you have to keep your promise to think about moving back permanently. You're my best friend and the thought of you not being around for my baby girl kills me. I want you in her life."

"That's a rotten thing to do, playing the baby card. It's going to take me at least another month to sort through Gus's stuff. I'm sure by then I'll have things figured out. But we're getting off-point here. You were filling me in on Mr. Hot Stuff."

Carly laughed. "Lord, he'd shit a brick if he heard you call him that. Every woman within a hundred square miles has tried to get his attention but it's like he's sworn off women for good. He's thirty-nine, same as Clay. His family moved here from South Dakota when he was sixteen, so we were only four or five. He joined the Marines right out of high school and stayed in for ten or so years. He refuses to talk about his time in the military, but Clay let it slip he had something to do with the Guantanamo detainees. Anyway, it was fairly soon after he got back from there that he left the military to join the Austin P.D. He did pretty well for himself there, made detective within a year. He started writing five years ago, got published right out of the gate and turned in his shield. When his daddy died eighteen months ago, Jace came back to run the ranch. He still writes, of course. I think his latest book was released last month."

"He's a writer?"

"Yep, prolific too. My high and mighty English teacher husband refers to his books as shank 'em and spank 'em, but I also know he keeps a stash of them hidden away."

"He writes porn?"

"Not exactly. He writes gritty soldier-of-fortune kinds of books but with an interesting subtext. His male protagonists are firm believers in Domestic Discipline."

A piece of lettuce lodged in Bri's throat and the resulting coughing jag drew the attention of everyone in the café, the last thing she wanted to do. "Domestic Discipline?"

Leaning forward as far as her belly would allow, Carly made her prissy face and whispered, "You know, that whole head-of-household thing where the man is king and rules the roost with an iron hand. Rumor has it that's what broke up his marriage. If you ask me, I think his ex did the right thing by getting out. I can't imagine why any woman in this day and age would let a man abuse her. If Tommy tried that crap with me, I'd pull a Bobbitt."

They were into dangerous territory and Bri chose her words carefully. "It's not abuse, Carly. From what I understand, it's almost always consensual." She laughed and wished she hadn't. It sounded forced because it was. "Don't look at me like that. One of my favorite erotic romance authors admits to being in the lifestyle. She writes about it in her blog."

In a dramatic gesture only Carly could pull off, she fanned herself with her hand. "You worried me there for a minute. Like you'd ever let a guy discipline you, Miss Independent. Where was I? Oh yeah, he and Clay went to high school together and over the years they've stayed in touch. Since Jace moved back, they're thick as thieves."

Bri glanced back out the window. The *thieves* had taken shelter from the afternoon sun beneath the overhang of Clay's hardware store. Chatting and laughing, Malone embodied every naughty thought she'd ever had, but she was still puzzled. None of the information imparted, while fascinating and not just a little disturbing, explained how she knew his name.

"He was with your granddad pretty much every day until the end, Bri. Jace gave the eulogy at his funeral. I sent you the newspaper clipping, remember?"

Recognition dawned first, followed quickly by guilt, her constant companion. Despite her granddad's protests, she should have come back to take care of him. Everything she had, everything she was she owed to him. At the very least, she should have found a way to make the funeral. Instead, she'd relinquished not only his care but his final farewell to well-meaning friends.

"Oops, I'm late. Doc Coleman warned me the next time I kept him waiting he was going to make me watch that film where that tiny woman gives birth to those three big babies. Gross." Grabbing her handbag, Carly stopped her slide across the bench seat. "You okay?"

So far from okay it was almost comical, she'd let her mask slip but put it quickly back in place with a bright smile and a nod. "I'm good. I'll see you tomorrow."

"No, you'll see me tonight. It's Friday and you promised to meet Tommy and me at Tiny's. That fiddler from San Antonio is coming back, the one I told you about."

"I'll think about it."

"Bri, the only time you leave that house is to have lunch with me and run some errands. That's not healthy. I know you're still grieving for Gus but it's been six months, and as far as feeling guilty about not being here, it wasn't like you had a choice. There may be a few people here who have a problem with it, but they don't know you like I do. My family adores you. When *Time* published your photographs from Afghanistan, Clay taped them up in the window of his hardware store. Make no mistake, I think you're nuts for running around the world like you do, but I'm proud of you and your granddad was too. You need to get back out there, hold that beautiful chin of yours high and show these yahoos what Augustus Shelton's grandbaby is made of."

Easier said than done. She was no longer sure what she was made of, but whatever it was, Gus wouldn't be proud. "You should have been a lawyer."

"That was the plan. Can you believe it? My last year of law school and Tommy knocks me up. See you tonight?"

"I'll be there."

Alone in the booth, Bri signaled the waitress for the check. As much as she wanted to take another peek across the street, she didn't dare. The last time she gazed that way, she was sure Malone caught her looking. Not that it was a crime to look out the window, and God knows there wasn't much else to look at. What she should do, and what her granddad would expect her to do, is walk across the street, look him in the eye and thank him. Whatever else he was, he'd been a friend to Gus when he needed one the most.

Her wallet open to pay the bill, she slipped the clipping from its nest. It was a little flowery and her granddad would have hated it, but it still made her proud.

*Serenity resident Jason Malone gave an eloquent eulogy for the man considered by many to epitomize the very best in Texas manhood. A former Texas Ranger, Augustus Shelton is survived by his grand-daughter, award-winning photographer Sabrina Shelton of Boston, Massachusetts.*

Award-winning jerk was closer to the truth.

# Chapter 2

Clay Edmonds closed the lid of the cooler and handed off a cold one to Jace.  "Not that I'm complaining, but I can't remember the last time you spent an hour shooting the bull with me in the middle of the day. You got writer's block or something? It wouldn't have anything to do with the pretty young thing across the street, would it?"

Hell yes, it had to do with her. The little prima donna had been back two weeks and not once had she tried to contact him. If she continued to ignore him, there'd be consequences. Forcing a grin, Jace tipped the bottle toward Clay. "Where I come from, we call that projecting. Maybe you need to hightail it up to Laredo, find a nice round woman and get your clock cleaned. The last few weeks you've been a little cranky."

"The last woman who cleaned my clock also cleaned my bank account, my 401K and ran off with my accountant. And for the record, you're not exactly the poster boy for sunshine and light yourself. You take a vow of celibacy I don't know about?"

"Nope, but it's a damn sight easier to create a beautiful woman on paper, spank her sweet ass and whack off in the shower. It's not perfect but I've still got my retirement fund."

The familiar tinkle of the café door got his attention and Jace's head popped up. Looking everywhere but at him, his quarry paused, turned on her heel and began the half block walk to her Jeep.

Behind him, Clay chuckled. "Speaking of sweet asses."

As tempting as it was to throw his buddy through the window of his own hardware store, Jace kept his cool. It was a sweet ass. Too bad it came attached to such a cold-hearted bitch. Slapping his thighs, he rose from the steps. "I need a few things inside and then I'm headed home."

Minutes later, as he was winding his way toward the front of the store, a female voice stopped him cold. It was coming from the porch, and unless he was mistaken, it was *her* voice. Soft and sexy like a caress, it grabbed his balls and squeezed, which was damn disconcerting to say the least. He was hoping it would be shrill and annoying, but Femi-Nazis were clever creatures, sweet as pie one minute and the Devil's own handmaiden the next. You couldn't trust them, especially the good-looking ones. Not that he gave a rat's-ass how attractive she was. He'd worked up quite a head of steam over her going on with her jet-setting life while Gus's was slipping away, and he knew just where to vent it. Lucky for him, he was immune to female wiles. *Once burned, twice shy* weren't just words. It was his personal creed, a creed in danger of going down the poop-chute when he ambled to the porch.

Looking better than any woman had a right to in worn jeans and a tank top, the brat laid a guilty little smile on him and extended her hand. "Mr. Malone, I'm Sabrina Shelton."

Ignoring the offer of a handshake, he leaned against a post and crossed his arms. "I know who you are. Gus had photographs of you all over his house. Your hair was longer." Short and stick straight, it suited her, but he'd been wrong about the color. Not just blond, it had the color and shine of finely-spun gold.

Clearly caught off-guard by the rebuff, she pulled her hand back and stuffed it in the pocket of her jeans. "I travel a lot and short hair is easier. I know what you did for my granddad, how close you were during his last few months. Thank you for that and for the eulogy."

"I sure as hell didn't do it for you."

Hovering like a mama bear protecting its cub, Clay blanched. "Jesus, Jace."

She caught her breath and for a second Jace feared he'd pushed too hard, but when she finally responded, she knocked him on his butt. "It's all right, Clay. There's nothing he could say to me that I haven't said to myself." She looked back up at him. "You don't know me but…"

"I know this much. Instead of sending you to those fancy schools, Gus should have kept you here and tanned your hide until you learned something about loyalty to family, not to mention manners."

Her large aquamarine eyes flashed anger and just as quickly softened in defeat. "Look, Mr. Malone, it's obvious you don't think much of me but my granddad made it clear he didn't want me here watching him die. He was a proud man, proud and stubborn, but I loved him very much and respected his wishes. When he passed, I was out of the country and couldn't get back. I'll have to live with the guilt for the rest of my life."

Her voice broke and before she could turn away, before he could scoop her up and run as far and fast as his legs would take them, big fat tears tumbled down her cheeks. Then she was gone. With a small shake of her head, she left the stoop and walked back the way she came.

Beside him, Clay growled, "Now look what you've done. I should kick your ass."

If he'd been able to, he would have kicked his own ass. Everything he thought he knew about Sabrina Shelton was a myth. Beneath the guise of daredevil tomboy and globe-trotting photographer, there was a young woman so full of pain it was palpable. "How long have you known her, Clay?"

"Since the day she was born so twenty-seven years give or take, why?"

"Gus once said he'd never known anyone quite as ready to take on the world as his granddaughter. He said she was born without the fear gene. Does that describe the woman who just left here?"

They watched her walk the last several yards to her Jeep. Head down and shoulders slumped forward, her body language radiated misery.

"Now that you mention it, I don't think I've ever seen her cry, not even when she came close to killing herself on that damn motorcycle. Carly said something the other day that surprised me too. She said Bri was considering moving back here, that she had one more assignment she was thinking of taking on and then she'd pack it in."

"Why the hell would she do that?" His jaw so tight, Jace thought it might snap.

"What's got your boxers in a bunch? You think if Carly knew she'd tell me? You know women. They talk a blue streak until you go fishing for information and then they clam up. Especially those two. They've had each other's backs since they were babies."

"She's in trouble, Clay."

"Christ, Jace, you've known the woman five minutes. What kind of trouble?"

"I'm not sure." He lied. He knew exactly what her trouble was. *I'll have to live with the guilt for the rest of my life.* No, she wouldn't, not if he had anything to say about it. Once he purged her of her guilt and whatever else was eating at her, he'd send her back to her glamorous life and he'd get on with his. The alternative was unthinkable. If her demons had their way and that pretty young thing moved back to Serenity, Jace Malone was a dead man.

# Chapter 3

Pushing back from the desk, Bri rolled her neck to work out the kinks. She'd been a mess when she returned from town. Confused and depressed, she stomped around the house for half an hour before powering up her laptop. Some six hours later, she was still confused and depressed, but now she added horny to the mix.

What started out as harmless curiosity had quickly devolved into fullblown obsession. Stopping only long enough to make a pot of coffee and pee, she'd devoured every website, every blog, anything and everything she could find on Domestic Discipline; and as if that weren't neurotic enough, she'd downloaded two ebooks dealing with the subject, hot as hell novellas that had her squirming in her chair.

She couldn't remember a time when she didn't know she was different and needed something outside the norm. The fantasies started in high school, daydreams in which a real man took her in hand, not some silly boy. It was when she got to college that a purloined copy of *The Story of O* clarified and narrowed her desires. She could admit to having submissive tendencies but masochism wasn't her thing. Degradation and torture for the sake of someone else's gratification struck her as a really bad deal. No way, Jose.

A visit to a Boston fetish club confirmed what she already knew but also muddied the waters. Though there was little doubt she enjoyed the spanking and after-care provided by the Dom, something was missing, something essential to who she was. The costumes and faux dungeon trappings made her feel more like a performer than a flesh and blood participant. Public displays, scripted responses and random partners were fine for those who got off on exhibitionism, but she wanted more.

Exactly what that was she hadn't known until today, but then words like cherished and cosseted hadn't been part of her lexicon either. Domestic Discipline filled the bill, one man who would love her but wasn't afraid to keep her in line, one man to put his foot down when the call of adventure reared its ugly head, one man who wouldn't feel the need to inflate his ego by destroying hers.

Oversimplification or not, she wanted it all. After Afghanistan, the sex might be a glitch, but with the right man she'd work through it. Problem was, the *right* man, the only man she'd let take her in hand was the one she couldn't have, the one who hated her guts. Not that she blamed him. Her earlier performance was far from stellar, so in addition to thinking her selfish and rude, he was probably convinced she was unhinged.

Maybe she was. Desperate to learn more about him, she'd cyber-stalked the poor guy. His website was a bust. Filled with raves about his books and the usual P.R. fluff, it received only a cursory glance before she moved on to the good stuff which, as luck would have it, turned out to be as far from good as it could get.

While she hoped to find that the former Mrs. Jason Malone was just a footnote in his life, such was not the case. Amazon tall and built like the proverbial brick outhouse, the auburn-haired Alyssa Prescott-Malone was a former Beauty Queen and a current prosecuting attorney with the Austin D.A.'s office. Citing irreconcilable differences, the couple had divorced just two years prior. By all accounts, the divorce was amicable and they continued to be *close*, a euphemism for *though the couple has agreed to go their separate ways, they reserve the right to get together on occasion and fuck each other's brains out.* Buxom Barbie and Kinky Ken. Love on steroids.

A lone coyote howled in the distance and she eased open the curtain, the imagery not lost on her. Dusk had always been her favorite time, a time of peace and renewal, but Gus's death and the ordeal of her last assignment changed all that. Now the night brought only sorrow, endless hours of regret.

As if to pull her from her dark thoughts, her cell phone chirped an incoming text but the reprieve was short-lived. She read it and winced.

*Get off your butt and move it or I'll sic JM on you. Carly*

The *JM* could only refer to one person which meant Clay spilled the beans. Now she was stuck. If she didn't go to Tiny's, the entire Edmonds clan would think she was in hiding. Her only choice was to suck it up and make an appearance. If Malone was there, so much the better. It was bad enough he thought she was wacky, but she'd be damned if she let him think she was a wimp.

Headed to the kitchen, she veered off toward the stairs. Food could wait. Still edgy from her *research*, she needed a hot shower and a nice long session with her vibrator. If she was going through with this, she wasn't going horny.

It was either the cool night air or the play date with her waterproof friend, but by the time she got to Serenity's one and only hot-spot, she'd worked through her obsession and was deep in *what was I thinking* mode. Caught up in the moment and vulnerable from her earlier encounter with Tall, Dark and Snarky, she'd let her emotions run away with her. The need to put a face to her fantasy led her straight to Jace Malone. And that road led to heartache.

# Chapter 4

From a table tucked away in a corner, Jace sensed her long before he saw her. It began as a subtle shift in energy, a change in the dynamic of the crowd, nothing he could put his finger on, but he knew she was there and so did every other person in the place.

When she finally came in view, it was obvious why so many male heads turned and female tongues clucked in disapproval. Dressed in low-slung jeans and a white shirt tied beneath her breasts, she looked good enough to eat, an image that took root in his brain and headed south.

She had guts; he'd give her that. Knowing full well there were others like himself who saw her absence as betrayal, she'd chosen a fair-sized gathering to make her first appearance. The former Texas Ranger had a lot of friends, some of them here, men and women alike who were waiting for the chance to rip the city girl to shreds. As much as he'd agreed with them before, it didn't sit well now. She was alone, adrift and hurting. What she needed was an anchor, a strong hand to guide her and get her back on course. A month at the outside, and he'd have her on her feet.

The one place he wouldn't have her is in his bed. Sex was off the table, no way, no how. One sip of her sweet nectar would be poison and that way lay madness. He wasn't a kid and this wasn't his first rodeo. At thirty-nine, he was wise enough to know he could admire a filly without riding her. His head was rational. It was his dick that had to get with the program.

"Mr. Malone?"

In the middle of chugging his beer, he almost choked. She got the drop on him that time, but it would be the last. In no hurry to acknowledge her, he looked her up and down. "Something you want, Sabrina?"

She blinked as a pretty blush touched her cheeks. "Have you seen Carly? She sent me a text about an hour ago."

"More like two hours ago. Tommy took her home. She wasn't feeling well. Nothing serious, she'll be fine."

"*You're a doctor too?*" He arched an eyebrow and she did that thing women do when they sense they're in trouble. She bit her lip, looked around the room and changed the subject. "I guess I missed the entertainment."

He finished off his beer, set the bottle on the table and fixed her with a look that said her subterfuge hadn't worked. "I guess." When she didn't run from the table, he pressed the advantage. "I'm going to grab a cup of coffee before heading home. Can I get you something from the bar?"

Her eyes widened like he'd just offered her a puppy and he bit back a groan. He imagined several scenarios for bringing back that look but one lingered a mite too long. She was naked in his bed, her hands clutching the headboard as he licked every inch of her velvet soft skin. If he wasn't careful, that look would be his downfall.

"A lite beer, please. In a bottle with the cap on."

Her zinger caught him halfway out of the chair. "That an East Coast thing or do you seriously believe I'm going to slip you a roofie?"

She flinched and he felt like an asshole. He'd seen what happened to women who didn't use good sense and here he was criticizing one who did. He blamed his ego. It wasn't one bit happy she thought he had to resort to drugs to get laid, but before she could utter a reply, he did that thing men do when they know they've been a douche bag. He lied through his teeth. "That was a joke, Sabrina. Have a seat."

With the bar behind her and slightly to the left, he could watch her unobserved. He finally grinned, something he hadn't allowed himself to do in her presence. Damned if she wasn't adorable, but other than a perp in an interrogation room, he'd never seen anyone so jumpy.

The little cat had claws too, a fact not lost on his cock. You're a doctor too? His grin broadened. He'd missed that the first time around. Sonofabitch if the little brat hadn't been doing some homework. He'd intended to wait a few days, run out to her place on some pretense or other and get her talking, maybe even find an excuse to paddle her ass, but when opportunity knocked, a man had to be a fool not to open the door. Stepping away from the bar with the coffee and beer, he turned back around, got the bartender's attention and made a slight adjustment. It was time to see how sharp those claws really were.

# Chapter 5

She was having a drink with him? In what parallel universe was that possibly a good idea? In the last eight hours, the man had not only ripped her a new one and made her cry, but he'd taken center stage in her Technicolor daydream.

He hadn't gotten any uglier either. Swapping his earlier duds for a pair of black butt-hugging jeans and turtleneck, his hair was held at the nape of his neck with some hammered silver thing, probably Native American. On any other man, it might have come across effeminate but on him it looked sexy as hell. She, on the other hand, could have walked in nude and he wouldn't have noticed. Clearly, she wasn't a beauty contest winner and her boobs were far from bodacious but give a girl a break. Would it have killed him to smile?

She peered around the noisy bar. He was just like all the rest. When she first walked in, she'd tried to engage a few people, mostly older folks, but they weren't smiling either, wouldn't even meet her eyes. She knew it would be hard coming back, but she was a fool to think it could be permanent. To all but a few, she would always be *that Shelton girl*, the little orphan taken in by her granddad and sent to all those *fancy* schools, the ingrate who put her career before family. The stories would go on from there, how she'd always been a problem, more boy than girl with her motorcycle and galavantin' all over the world.

"There you go."

She looked at the bottle of soda and then up at Jace. "Thank you but I wanted a beer."

"I heard you, but you're not getting a beer. It's a twenty minute drive back to your place and I don't like the idea of you driving impaired."

"I make it in fifteen, ten if I floor it." Popping the cap with a church key from her pocket, she morphed her saccharine smile to a glare. "Butt out, Malone."

"Jace."

"Excuse me?"

"I let all the women I make cry call me Jace."

She just bet he did and if that was supposed to be an apology, it sucked. "Don't flatter yourself. I'm PMS-ing. You're lucky I didn't shoot you."

His laughter brought on the return of a bone-melting crush. Low and husky like his voice, it was a great laugh, the kind she'd had too little of in her life.

"How'd the research go today?"

Thankful she wasn't in mid-gulp, she felt the flush start in her toes and work its way up. "I don't know what you're talking about."

"Sure you do. I was a detective for five years and before that a Special Forces interrogator. Your eyes are red and you've been rolling your shoulders and flexing the fingers of your right hand. I'm guessing you were on your computer for, what, six hours?"

"You're creepy."

"You were eyeballing me pretty good while you were having lunch with Carly. She give you an earful?"

"Creepy and arrogant. Tonight's my lucky night."

"Could be, honey. What'd you have in mind?"

Dropping her jaw, she stared at him a good ten seconds before she got a full-on case of giggles. She couldn't have stopped them if her life depended on it, and the sterner he looked, the worse they got. When she finally composed herself, she swiped at her eyes. "Sorry."

"Something funny you want to share, Sabrina?"

"It occurred to me that if I walk behind the bar I'll find your shriveled-up corpse, the real Jace Malone, the one we all knew before the aliens replaced you with a pod-person."

His grin was as sexy as the rest of him, the slow-burning kind that put a sizzle in her panties and scorched a hole through her resolve. "*Invasion of the Body Snatchers*, Kevin McCarthy and Dana Wynter, 1956."

"Donald Sutherland, Brooke Adams and Jeff Goldblum, 1978, although I tend to agree that the black and white version was better. The other two remakes aren't worth mentioning. Please don't tell me you're a fan of old sci-fi films, Malone. It's going to be so much harder to hate you."

"I was thinking the same about you, Shelton."

Rattled by the unexpected by-play, she was grateful for the vibration of her cellphone and snuck a peek at the display. "It's Carly. I'll take it outside." Her heart racing a mile a minute, her palms so sweaty that she almost dropped the phone, she sucked in a few breaths of fresh air before pressing the 'talk' button. "You okay? Jace said Tommy took you home."

"Oh my God, Bri, are you there with him now?"

"I'm not answering any questions until you tell me why you left."

"Tommy said I looked tired, and the next thing I knew we were in his pick-up headed home. Where are you right this minute?"

"I'm outside, why?"

"Where's Jace?"

"He's inside. Are you having some kind of prenatal meltdown?"

"Shut up for a second and listen to this. 'Somewhere north of cute and south of drop-dead gorgeous, she had a face he liked to look at, heartshaped, with enormous blue-green eyes and a small, upturned nose. Punctuated by a single freckle above her upper lip, her mouth was in a class all its own. Full and pouty, it was a mouth that inspired poems, songs and more than a few male fantasies. And damn, wouldn't it just figure her body was the kind he preferred. On the tiny side, five foot five at best, she was curvy in all the places a woman should be curvy — high, perky breasts, a tiny waist, and the sweetest ass this side of Heaven. Her blonde hair hit her shoulders…' It goes on from there but you get it, right?"

"I get that you need to inhale a pint of Ben & Jerry's and call me in the morning."

"It's you, goofball. When I got home, I wasn't ready to go to sleep so I happened to pick up the book Tommy's reading and, holy shit, I almost gave birth on the sofa."

"Carly…"

"It's Jace's latest book and right here on page forty-two he's described you to a T, everything, right down to that tiny mole to the left of your upper lip. Are you sure you never met him before today? This is too weird."

Weird didn't begin to describe it but writers did that kind of thing, drew from actual events and people, didn't they? *Gus had photographs of you all over his house.* "It's probably a coincidence but do me a favor and don't mention this to anyone, especially Tommy or Clay. We're just starting to be civil to one another and I don't want anyone razzing him about it, okay?"

"How civil?"

"Not that civil. Pinky promise?"

"Jeez, Bri, what are we, five?"

"Carly?"

"Oh, all right. Pinky promise but I don't think it's very nice you're forcing me to keep something this juicy from Baby Daddy."

"If you'd kept your juicy something from Baby Daddy in the first place, you'd be studying for the Bar exam. Just sayin'."

The phone call ended but she had the uneasy feeling her best friend had opened a can of worms and left her to deal with the squirmy little buggers. It would be a mistake to read too much into Jace's dead-on description, an even bigger mistake to believe he thought of her as anything beyond a nuisance. They'd shared a moment, a mutual fondness for a certain type of film, nothing more.

Or was it? She had two options, call the night a win, get in her car and go home or face the situation head-on. Bewitched and not just a little bewildered, she looked back toward the door. Maybe she was screwed up, but what if he was the one destined to carry her off into the sunset and love her and keep her safe? It was a conundrum—not to mention sudden—but then as if some invisible force was at play, each and every argument she'd had with herself over the previous few hours dissolved into a blinding haze of need. Of all the mistakes she could make, by far the worst would be walking away without knowing.

She didn't think she was gone that long, but by the time she opened the doors and took a few steps back inside, she was shocked to find that most of the patrons had cleared out. A glance at the table in the corner confirmed what she already knew. The drinks were there but Jace had seized the moment and vamoosed. She'd been so caught up in the phone call and her silly delusions, he probably passed right by her on the way to his car.

What few people remained were standing at the bar, older men and women her granddad's age, some she recognized, others not. She nodded and smiled, but like a lynch mob in a B-movie Western, they looked angry as they advanced on her. Fighting the impulse to turn tail and run, she held her ground and acknowledged the one in front, the one she knew best and liked the least. "How are you, Mr. Fields?"

"I'll be a lot better once I've had my say. You know, when your daddy and mama ran off and got themselves killed, a lot of us, me and the missus included, thought Gus ought to put you in a foundling home. We told him you'd grow up to be wild like your folks. Gus wouldn't listen, said you were family and family took care of their own. Now here you are proving us right. It burns my ass that you come sashayin' in here six months after he's dead. Gus was my friend and…"

"Stop it! Just stop." Reminded of an earlier confrontation, this time she refused to retreat. "How dare you call yourself a friend! You can say whatever you want about me but you know very well my folks didn't run off. They were part of a search and rescue team looking for a group of missing kids when their plane went down. Gus loved them and was proud of them and a true friend wouldn't denigrate their memory or his by talking trash about them."

Movement at the edge of the group grabbed her eye and what little hold she had on reality shattered. The face looking back at her was dark and familiar, a mask of rage like all the others. Holding it together by a thread, she put one foot in front of the other until she was out the door. And then she ran.

Choking back sobs, she fell hard when her feet lost purchase on the gravel, but she picked herself up and bounded for the Jeep. When she was close enough to touch it, a muscled arm came out of nowhere and pulled her against a rock-hard chest. "Easy, tiger, I've got you."

Her body stiffened, and the instant he loosened his hold, she pushed away from him and hissed, "Don't touch me. And you can go back inside and tell your friends I won't be sashaying into any of your lives again." Frantically searching her pockets for keys, she groaned when she remembered where she left them.

"Is this what you're looking for?" Just beyond her reach, Jace dangled them from his fingers. "I picked them up off the table when I went to the head, which is where I was when that asshole shot his mouth off." He took a step toward her and lifted her chin. "I don't believe in doing things by committee. If I have something to say to you, and I'm pretty sure I'll have a lot to say to you before this night is over, I'll do it in private. Now get in the car."

She wasn't sure which surprised her more, the actual words or the fact that he could speak them between clenched teeth. "May I have my keys, please?"

"You're not driving upset. I'll take you home."

"That's not necessary."

"I don't like repeating myself, Sabrina. That's something you should know right off."

If she'd had her wits about her, she would have flipped him off or saluted. Instead, she threw open the passenger door and buckled herself in. By the time they hit the main road, her adrenalin was spent and the shakes were setting in. To make matters worse, the knee she'd fallen on was starting to sting and throb like crazy. Embarrassed by a fresh wave of tears, she wrapped her arms around herself and turned her face toward the side window.

"What did that old fool say to you?"

"Nothing you haven't said but at least you didn't bring my folks into it. I know their type. They figure since they're such decent church-going, Godfearing folks they can say whatever they want and get away with it. Just once, I'd like to see Jesus come down and slap them into next week."

"Aside from needing to dumb-down your vocabulary, you did a pretty fair job of slapping them yourself. And just so you know, I'm not one bit happy you thought I was part of that ambush."

Her nerves shot and frustration bubbling right below the surface, she faced him and frowned. "You're right. I forgot how gracious you were this afternoon when I tried to thank you. And just so *you* know, I don't give a flying fuck how happy you are."

Tightening his hands on the steering wheel, he trumped her frown with a scowl. "That's some mouth you've got on you. When was the last time you got your butt blistered?"

"When was the last time you were arrested for assault and battery? Tell me something, Malone. Does that caveman crap work on Austin girls or do you think because I was born in Podunk Central, I'm not going to call you on your macho bullshit?"

He got that look again, the one that hardened her nipples and turned her pussy into pulp. "Shelton, you don't want to know what I think. Now answer the question. Has a man ever put you over his knee, pulled down your britches and wailed the tar out of you, because I don't think I've ever met a woman who needed it worse."

If she'd learned anything from living on the South Texas Plains, it was that poking a nest of rattlesnakes was just plain dumb. On the other hand… "Not that it's any of your business, but the last time I had my butt blistered was my twenty-fifth birthday. Master Julian…"

The screech of brakes was followed by a hard right turn and long moments of sheer panic. When she opened her eyes, Jace had pulled the Jeep to the side of the road and was grinning at her, a grin way more irritating than sexy. "Master Julian? *You* went to a BDSM club?"

"No, it was fetish night at *Chuck E. Cheese*. What's so damn funny?"

"Picturing you as a submissive. You're about as submissive as a herd of rampaging rhinos."

A lot he knew. There was something seriously wrong with her. Ten minutes ago, she wanted to flay him with a potato peeler and now she was ready to jump him. It was one thing to sit across from him in a noisy bar but the confines of the Jeep put him way too close for comfort. He smelled like heaven. Correction. He smelled like sin, not that it would do her any good. As for the session with her vibrator, she might as well have used the time to paint her nails.

# Chapter 6

Well, damn. That was another image he could do without, her sweetheart of an ass all red and tingly from another man's hand. It was a good thing sex was off the menu. The only thing he liked better than spanking a spitfire was bedding her afterward, and with his cock as hard as a railroad spike, she might not survive it.

He got the Jeep back on the road and stared straight ahead, debating his options. The plan, which turned out to be not so much a plan as an impulse, was to drop her at her place, check the house to make sure everything was secure and call one of the hands to pick him up. Now that just didn't seem right. On top of everything else she was dealing with, she'd probably fret all night about old man Fields shooting his mouth off. Judging by the hint of dark circles beneath her pretty eyes, she couldn't afford many more sleepless nights.

She couldn't afford to miss many more meals either. Photographs might add a few pounds but she was a good ten pounds thinner than the last one Gus had shown him, and with her small frame, that was too much. Women were meant to have curves. If he wanted to hug a clothes hanger, he had a closet full of them.

*Whoa.* Where did that come from? There'd be no hugging. Or kissing. That one hurt. Hands down, she had the most kissable lips he'd ever seen in his life. No spanking either, not tonight. Correction was done on the bare, and though he considered his willpower above average, he was in no mood to test it.

Knowing full well he was going to regret it, he drove past the road to Gus's and waited for the inevitable explosion. When it didn't come, he figured she thought he'd get out at his place and let her drive the last couple of miles alone. It was as good a time as any to disabuse her of that notion. "You're staying at my place tonight."

She tensed but her response threw him for a loop, her voice so soft and sad it might have broken his heart, assuming he had one. "Don't I at least get pizza and a movie first?"

"You might if I were intending to put the moves on you, which I'm not. What you need is a friend, not a lover. First I'm going to bandage your knee and then I'm going to fix you something to eat. When was the last time you had a decent meal?"

She still wasn't looking at him, and in answer to his question, she shook her head.

"That's what I thought. You've lost too much weight and I know you're not getting enough sleep, something else we'll work on."

That did it. If looks could kill, he'd be deader than the armadillo he just swerved to avoid. "You know, Malone, I've read Gus's will and I don't recall seeing anything in it about you being appointed my guardian. I appreciate your concern, but I want to go home."

"It wasn't multiple choice, Sabrina."

The moon was low and bright enough to see those aquamarine slits leveled at him. As much as he liked fire and spirit in a woman, and in his bed, those looks would have to go. He was a stickler for respect, but he didn't believe in belaboring the point with words. There were far more effective ways to deal with bad behavior, and he was going to enjoy the hell out of introducing her to them. Before the month was out, she'd know the sting of his hand and his belt, and if he could fix her in the process, so much the better.

# Chapter 7

She wanted to crawl into a hole and pull the whole damn world on top of her. Her snippy retort hit the nail on the head. It all made sense, the mixed signals, the solicitous way he insisted on driving her home, even his concern for her health. Gus had asked him to look after her.

No matter how far she travelled or how many accolades she amassed, she'd always be a kid to her granddad. Oddly enough, it wasn't his posthumous prying that rankled as much as his choice of a nursemaid. The worst part was how easy she'd made it for Malone by falling in lust at first sight. He was probably getting off on her crush. The man wasn't stupid. He had to know the effect he had on her, and Lord knows she was ripe for the picking. For a brief happy moment at Tiny's, she took the bait hook, line and sinker.

In deference to Gus, she'd play along, but only to a point. She'd let him fix her leg, maybe even feed her, but she drew the line at spending the night. Appearances to the contrary, she had her pride. Now, thanks to the events of the day and Gus's meddling, she had something else, a renewed determination to leave Serenity for good and never look back.

The Jeep cleared the iron gates and her first view of the Triple M Ranch pitched her forward in the seat. Lined on both sides with a variety of lush low-hanging trees, the quarter-mile-long driveway ended in front of a home that belonged on the cover of *Architectural Digest*. Artfully lighted inside and out to optimize the impact, the handsome old Victorian appeared to have been beautifully restored, everything from the stained glass windows to the deep, wraparound porch. She was still ogling the structure when he brought the Jeep to a stop and turned off the ignition. "It's magnificent, Jace. Did you restore it?"

"My folks did. It took them fifteen years. When they bought it in the late eighties, the roof was falling in and there wasn't a window in the place. The last stained glass window, the red one over the door, was installed a week before my mother passed away."

It was a small peek inside his heart but at least he had one. She was beginning to wonder. "I'm sorry."

"I guess I don't have to tell you anything about losing parents."

"I was only nine months old when they died. You can't miss what you never had."

Their eyes locked and by the muted glow of the porch light she saw the same heat she'd seen at Tiny's. Only this time she wasn't buying it. Opening the vehicle door, she faked a breezy tone to accompany the plastic smile. "Let's go, Doc Malone. I'd like to see inside before I bleed to death."

The interior was equally impressive. Off the welcoming foyer was a parlor, a study and a dining room, all tastefully decorated. Wood was polished to within an inch of its life, metals gleamed and even the stamped copper ceiling looked pristine and new.

Directly in front of her, the stairwell wall was chock-a-block with family photos, but one in particular pulled her in. It had to be his parents. A shade darker than Jace, his father looked enough like him to be his twin. They had similar builds and the same rugged good looks. The woman was younger and stunning, a petite little thing with fiery red hair and alabaster skin.

Jace walked up behind her and stood so close she swore she could feel his heart beating against her back. "My mom and dad."

"They were a beautiful couple. How did they meet?"

"Dad was a tribal cop on the Pine Ridge Reservation. Mom was at Yale in the doctoral program for Criminal Justice. She went to South Dakota to get background for her thesis on Leonard Peltier. She was hell-bent on proving he was getting a raw deal."

"He did get a raw deal."

"You know something about that case, do you?"

Annoyed at the condescending tone in his voice, she turned and looked up at him, ticking off the items on her fingers. "I know the FBI presented the Canadian authorities with fraudulent documents to get him sent back to the U.S. I know key defense witnesses were banned from testifying. I know the ballistics evidence was squirrely at best, but all attempts to get that fact before the jury were ruled inadmissible. I know there wasn't a single eyewitness who could place Peltier anywhere near the scene of the crime. And I also know law enforcement. Two cops were killed and someone was going to pay, guilty or not. Anything else you want to know, Detective Malone?"

He raised a hand as if he were going to touch her but thought better of it and dropped it back to his side. "You stumble on that story when you were doing your research on me?"

Stopping short of jabbing his chest with her finger, she lanced him with a glare. "For your information, I had a life before I met you, Malone, and part of that life included an interest in seeing that people wrongly incarcerated were given an opportunity to clear themselves. I've been making small donations to *The Innocence Project* since high school. The prisons are full of people who languish there for years because cops and prosecutors care more about keeping up their conviction rate than getting to the truth." There, she said it, and if he could read between the lines, he'd know exactly what she thought of him, the justice system in general and his ex-wife in particular.

His eyebrows shot up as a smile tweaked his way-too-tempting mouth. "I wouldn't have taken you for a crusader."

"The sheer volume of what you don't know about me is staggering," she snapped before inclining her head toward the photograph. "So what's the rest of their story?"

"A lot of people on the reservation weren't happy about her being there and asking questions. Some even thought she was undercover for the Feds. Dad decided it was in everyone's best interest if she went back to New Haven, so he drove to where she was staying and packed her bags for her. He was about to put her in his car and haul her to the airport when she took exception to what she perceived as heavy-handed treatment and broke a table lamp over his head. When he came to, his own gun was pointed at him. He wrestled it away from her, paddled her ass and married her a week later."

Lord help her, she'd reached a new low, envying a dead woman. "I guess heavy-handed worked for her, huh?"

"I guess." This time when he lifted his hand, he followed through and tucked some errant strands of hair behind her ear. "The first-aid kit is in the kitchen." He hitched his thumb to the rear of the house. "Thataway."

If she thought the rest of the house was charming, the kitchen took the cake. Outfitted with every modern convenience, it was bright and airy and period-appropriate. "This is amazing. Do you cook?"

"Mostly I defrost, but I know my way around a microwave. My foreman's wife takes care of most of the cooking and looking after the house. Take your jeans off."

Great segue but she wasn't taking anything off, least of all her jeans. "Just cut them. They're ruined anyway. I'll turn them into shorts."

"That I'd like to see." His killer smile displayed a set of perfect white teeth. *All the better to eat you with, my dear.* "I was married, Sabrina. I've seen a woman in her panties. As matter of fact, I've pretty much seen it all."

She didn't doubt that for a minute, but panties didn't exactly describe what she was wearing. Her thong was the size of a thumbnail and sopping wet to boot, evidence of her traitorous libido. "Look, Jace…"

"What did I tell you about not liking to repeat myself? Drop 'em."

It was hard to keep up. One minute he was flirting with her and the next he'd gone all badass cop. She needed a scorecard. Or a gun.

On second thought, it didn't matter what he thought of her. After tonight, she planned to avoid him like the plague. She was leaving in a month anyway, maybe sooner if she could get her act together. She'd already decided to skip the culinary portion of the evening. After he bandaged her leg, and while he was feeling all warm and fuzzy about his good deed, she'd find an excuse to go to the Jeep, use the spare key under the wheel well and hightail it home. A plan in hand, she unzipped her jeans and wiggled them to the floor. "You're bossy, you know that?"

"Honey, you don't know the half of it." Oh so slowly, his eyes roved over every inch of her before settling on the thong. "I take back what I said about seeing it all. I don't think I've ever seen anything like that."

Beyond embarrassed, she rolled her eyes skyward. "Can we just get this over with?"

This time she wasn't imagining it. The only thing hotter than the impressive bulge in his jeans was his expression of appreciation, which might well have singed off the rest of her clothes had he not chosen that moment to encircle her waist and hoist her to the countertop. His touch was gentle as he cleaned the wound but the antiseptic burned like blazes and brought tears to her eyes. Grabbing on to his shoulders, she bit her lip.

Never in a month of Sundays did she expect what happened next. He leaned in close, his breath warm and minty on her cheek. "My turn."

It was just a nibble at first and then it was something else, something she wanted so badly she whimpered. His mouth took possession of hers, his tongue teasing, exploring, a full-out assault on her senses. As her body responded, she wrapped her arms around his neck. Desperate to connect, she spread her legs and thrust her hips forward.

That ended the kiss. Peeling her arms from around his neck, he stepped back, the heat absent from his eyes, nothing there but cold resolve plus a trace of something she couldn't decipher. "We need to talk."

Talk? The very last thing she wanted to do was talk. What kind of game was he playing? Whatever it was, it was exhausting. He was exhausting. And she was pathetic. She should just get out of there before she made an even worse fool of herself. Unfortunately, once again her curiosity got the best of her. "Talk about what?"

"I've been around enough cases of PTSD to know you have more than your fair share of symptoms. I think that's why you're thinking of moving back. What happened to you?"

For the second time in as many hours, her world went sideways. She jumped down from the counter, kicking any pretense of civility to the curb. "Save your vivid imagination for your books, Malone. I'm a human being, not a storyline. I'm not your project either, so the next time you feel compelled to mentor someone, try the Boys and Girls Club. I loved Gus dearly but he had no right to foist me on you and vice versa."

"What are you talking about? Gus has nothing to do with us."

He seemed genuinely bewildered by her outburst, but she'd sooner chew nails than get sucked in again. "Us? Is that a joke or some ploy you picked up in *Psychology for Dummies*? I'm going home."

Bending down to pick up her jeans, she had the air pulled out of her as he snared her around the waist and carried her from the kitchen. "The hell you are. You're going over my knee which is where you should have been hours ago."

Too shocked to do much more than thrash around, she used the only weapon at her disposal. "Cocksucker! You put me down, Jace Malone. You don't have a right…"

"I have every right. I'm going to spank that sass right out of you and then we're going to have a chat."

She still hadn't caught her breath when she found herself manhandled over his lap in the study. He didn't believe in warm-ups, that much was obvious. His hand came down and beat a merciless tattoo on first one cheek then the other. Within seconds, she was sobbing. "Stop, Jace, it hurts!"

"Damn right it hurts and it's going to hurt a lot more before I'm finished with you, and if I ever hear you use language like that again, you won't be able to sit down for a year."

True to his word, he kept on spanking her until she thought she was going to die. He finished up by landing a few nasty slaps to her upper thighs. By the time he lifted her to her feet, she was dazed and shaken to her core. "I hate you."

"Yeah, I can tell."

She wanted to hate him, she really did, but as the silence roared between them, she knew that wasn't going to happen. She felt swollen all over, and achy, and wet. In her entire life, nothing ever hurt that badly, and she'd happily go through it again if he would just hold her, but that wasn't happening either.

His dark eyes narrowed and she thought she saw pain, maybe conflict, like he was afraid to make the first move. Before she could chicken out, she untied the knot below her breasts and shrugged out of the blouse. Standing before him in a skimpy bra and thong, she'd never felt more exposed. Or terrified.

To her horror and humiliation, he shook his head. "That's far enough." Rising from the wingback, he handed her the jeans she'd dropped and then the blouse. "There's a guest room upstairs, first door on your left. You'll find extra towels in the adjoining bathroom. We'll talk in the morning."

Fighting back a fresh onslaught of tears, she slipped on the blouse and stepped into the jeans. "I don't think so. Whatever self-respect I have left after today, I'd like to hold on to it." She walked to the door, afraid he'd stop her but more afraid he wouldn't. When he didn't, she summoned her last bit of courage. "There's someone else, isn't there?"

"It's not you, Sabrina."

Her hand on the doorknob, she squeezed her eyes shut. "I know I'm not the one, Jace. I got that message loud and clear. Thanks for the triage and the spanking, but I think I'll stick with fetish clubs. At least there, people know what they want."

# Chapter 8

Jace scrubbed a hand over his face and blew out his breath. *It's not you, Sabrina.* Brilliant. For a wordsmith, he'd mucked that up to a fare-theewell. He may have spanked her ass, but she did a damn fine job of nailing his.

It was no worse than he deserved. Twice in one day she'd shown him her heart and both times he'd rejected her and reduced her to tears. The only winner was Alyssa, who'd be doing cartwheels if she knew how badly she screwed him up. That he'd never loved her and married her out of a sense of obligation didn't alter the cost of her betrayal. He couldn't change the past, but by allowing it to dictate his future, he wasn't just a coward but a fool.

He'd fought the good fight and lost. In spite of all his protestations, he'd fallen for the hellcat, fallen hard and fast. Gus tried to tell him of her intelligence, her humor and compassion but the words fell on deaf, angry ears. It was easier and safer to see her as a villain. Little did he know that in a single day she would trample his preconceptions into dust, that her departure would cut him to the quick. Tantrums and hysterics he could deal with, but there were no Drama Queen theatrics, no slamming of doors or tires spitting gravel on the driveway. In that same soft, sexy voice, she said her piece and walked out of his life.

Or so she thought. She was everything he never knew he wanted and there was no way he was letting her go. Running after her tonight would be a mistake. She needed to cool off and he needed to cool down. He'd give her the weekend, but come Monday, that sweet young thing was his.

# Chapter 9

"I figured I'd find you here. What the fuck did you do to Bri?"

Jace jerked his head toward the door of Clay's store and saw a hundred fifty pounds of perturbed pregnant woman bearing down on him. Not exactly the way he'd planned to start his day. "Did she tell you I did something to her?"

"Don't you dare try to weasel out of this, Jace. I want to know right here and now what you did to her. I figured she was busy when she blew me off for lunch Saturday and Sunday, but today's Monday and no one's seen hide nor hair of her since the two of you met up at Tiny's. I talked to her that night and she said you were getting on fine, but when I drove out to her place today, she was…perky." Carly threw up her hands. "Perky!"

"Carly, calm down." More than a little befuddled by his sister's melodrama, Clay turned to Jace. "Maybe I'm missing something but perky is a good thing, isn't it? Hell, you're the writer. Doesn't perky mean the same as happy?"

Jace shrugged. If he knew women, Carly wasn't done, not by a long shot, and he wanted to hear her out. His next stop was Gus's and he needed to know what he was walking into. "Go on, Carly. You know her better than anyone."

"Damn right I do. Where was I?"

"Perky."

"Right. Bri's not like everyone else. The last time I saw her perky was right after Billy Thomas told her he'd rather kiss the ass end of an armadillo than her. He said it in front of everyone at the Founder's Day dance. She was ten. Even back then she didn't want anyone to know how hurt she was. No one saw her for the rest of the summer. But that's not the worst of it. She's got that sleazy realtor Frank Parsons from Middleton going out there today. She's selling the ranch and everything in it, everything, right down to the contents. She's going back to Boston for good and she's cutting ties with everyone here, including me. I worked on her for days getting her to consider coming back here and you ruined it in one damn night. You don't know what it took for her to go to Tiny's and be around people again. She's been holed up in her apartment for months, ever since the doctors released her and they flew her back from…oh, hell."

His stomach clenched as bile gurgled up in his throat. "Flew her back from where and why was she under a doctor's care?" He looked at Clay. "What do you know about this?"

"It's the first I've heard of it." After making sure they were alone in the store, Clay turned the *open* sign to *closed*. "Start talking, sis."

"She'll kill me, Clay. You know how proud she is. She wouldn't tell me the whole story, but what she told me was bad enough. It was the night before she was supposed to come back to the states from Afghanistan. A few of her fellow journalists wanted to give her a send-off so they invited her to one of their rooms. There were some men there she didn't know, and she felt funny about it but stayed because the party was for her. Someone slipped some GHB into her soda and she had a bad reaction, real bad. She was in a coma for three weeks. She woke up in a hospital in London and from there was flown back to Boston. That's the reason she didn't make Gus's funeral. She was sick for months but didn't tell me for fear word would get back to him while he was dying."

Cold rage and guilt, the worst he'd ever known, threatened to bring Jace to his knees. "Was she raped?"

"That's the worst part. She can't remember a thing and wherever they took her first, the doctors were too busy trying to diagnose her. By the time they figured out what it was, it was too late to collect any samples. I know she went to a doctor in Boston and insisted on a battery of tests for STDs. The tests all came back negative but, God, can you imagine not knowing?"

He couldn't imagine any of it, including her going through it alone. It had to be hell, waiting for the test results and grieving over Gus. All the signs were there but he'd missed the most important one. *Do you seriously believe I'm going to slip you a roofie?* If he hadn't been such a horse's ass and spent more time listening and less time trying to deny his feelings for her, he might have seen her request not as an indictment but a clue. Bad things happened to good girls every day, but the idea that someone could get away with almost killing her made his blood boil.

"You fix this, Jace. I want my baby girl to know my best friend. She's brave and honest and funny."

"You're preaching to the choir, Carly. I know what she is." *She's mine.* Carly was still sniffling when he took her by the shoulders. "I want you to pay attention because this is important. We never had this discussion. She can never know you told me, got it?"

She nodded. "That's one secret I will definitely keep. What are you going to do?"

"I need to make a few phone calls and then I'm going after my woman and bringing her home." If he wasn't still furious, the expressions on their faces might have made him laugh. For once, they were both speechless. He was too. Otherwise he might have spilled the rest of the story, one that surprised even him. *And then I'm going to marry her.*

# Chapter 10

Warily regarding his daughter above half-glasses, Gordon Prescott laced his hands together atop the antique mahogany desk. "You really want to have this discussion again?"

Alyssa Prescott-Malone flipped her hair and jiggled her Manolo-clad foot. "I want him back, Daddy. I haven't had a real man since he walked out on me, haven't had much of anything else either, if you get my meaning. All that stuff about everything being bigger in Texas is a bunch of bull. The men I've been seeing are just plain pitiful in the equipment department."

"Christ on the cross, girl, I haven't even had my first martini. The last thing I want to hear about is your sex life."

"But I need a favor and I don't have anywhere else to turn. I miss Jace. You said if I agreed to the divorce, he'd come running back."

"That was before I found out how you got him to the altar in the first place. You flat-out lied about having one in the oven. What the hell were you thinking?"

"It was the only way I could get him to marry me. Don't look at me like that, Daddy. You know how I get when I set my mind to something. I'm just like you." Flattery usually worked like a charm, but this time she wasn't so sure. He didn't look happy.

"Daughter, you're nothing like me. I didn't get where I am by making foolish decisions. You should have done your due diligence and not tried to pull a fast one on a man like Jason Malone. Now you tell me the truth. He never did try any of that funny stuff like you were spreading around, did he?"

"No. It was me that first brought it up to him. A month or two after the wedding, he figured out I wasn't pregnant and moved into the guest room. I thought it was temporary and he'd come back in my bed when he stopped being mad at me. Nine months later when he still hadn't touched me, I was getting desperate. The whole spanking thing sounded kinda sexy, so one night I had the cook make him a nice meal and I dressed up like a schoolgirl."

"I'm going to be real sorry for asking but what'd he do?"

"He said he wouldn't waste the energy. He said the kind of relationship he wanted wasn't about dressing up and play-acting. It was about two people trusting one another, and he couldn't trust me any further than he could throw me. That's when he gave me the choice of saving face and filing for divorce or he'd do it. I couldn't let that happen. I'd be the laughing stock of Austin."

"You're doing a pretty good job of that yourself. You've got the lowest conviction rate of anyone in the D.A.'s office. Do you have any idea how many favors I had to call in to get you that job, particularly since you didn't exactly distinguish yourself in Law School?"

"I know, but my heart's not in it. I could do better if I was happy and settled down with Jace. I've changed, Daddy, and I need to get close to him again to prove it. Will you help me?"

"That depends. Why is this the first time I'm hearing the truth, girl?"

"I was embarrassed. I mean, look at me. I could have any man, 'cept the one I want. I'm lonely too. I guess I could move back in with you and mama."

"What is it you want me to do?"

"Are you still friends with that man who owns the security firm, you know, the one who employs all those former military men?"

"What are you up to, Alyssa?"

"I was just thinking maybe someone could nose around and see what Jace's up to. I'm sure he doesn't have anyone else in his life, but I need to be sure before I put my plan in action. I want you to be proud of me again, like you were when I won all those pageants."

"I'll make a phone call but no more lying, you hear?"

"Cross my heart, Daddy. I'm a changed woman. I've learned my lesson."

# Chapter 11

What was this, Grand Central Station? Back two weeks and she hadn't had a single visitor. Now they were beating down her door.

Shielding her eyes from the sun, Bri peered down the private road.

Someone was hauling ass and kicking up dust. It wasn't Carly. *Thank you, Jesus.* As much as she loved the woman, she couldn't take another inquisition. Carly drove like an old man, a drunk, blind old man, and whoever was behind the wheel of this vehicle knew a thing or two about cars and a whole lot about speed. He must be doing eighty. Where did he think he was, the Indy 500?

"You expecting someone, honey?"

*Honey?* Frank Parsons was starting to get on her nerves, the ones not already frayed by Friday night's fiasco. Talk about stereotypes. Parsons gave salesmen a bad name with his over-whitened teeth and grubby paws. He wasn't there five minutes when he found an excuse to touch her shoulder and arm. If he tried it again, he'd lose a hand. Her place was remote, out in the middle of nowhere, so maybe it wasn't such a bad idea to have someone hang around for a spell, at least until she got rid of Texas' answer to Austin Powers.

Then again, maybe not. There was only one person in the county with the balls to drive an Escalade when everyone else had pick-ups, the same damn fool she'd spent the weekend cursing up and down and trying to forget. What was he doing here? Never mind. She didn't care why he was here. She just cared that he left. Post-haste. And if he expected to find her teary and miserable, he had another thing coming. She might cry her eyes out when he left, but while he was here, it was show time.

Squaring her shoulders, she waited till he alighted from the Escalade before blasting him with a smile. "Well, Jace Malone, I was just talking about you."

"Were you now?" He swaggered toward her, a big grin on his face.

Her knees went weak and her throat was so dry she could have coughed up a fur ball. Yeah, she was over him. "Frank was asking about the boxes on the porch and I told him they were for you. It's stuff I thought Gus would want you to have, seeing as how you and he were so close and all. It's not much, his old service revolver, a chess set and some books. I was going to have Clay run them out to your place the next time I saw him. I'm sorry. Do you two know one another? Jace Malone, Frank Parsons. I was showing Frank around the place before I sign the listing."

"Take a breath, sweetheart. You going somewhere?"

*Sweetheart?* She was so knee-deep in bullshit she was tempted to reach for a shovel. "I'm going back to Boston and from there it's anybody's guess, Europe maybe."

Burning a hole through her with those sinful brown eyes, Jace thumbed back his Stetson. "Mr. Parsons, I'm going to have to ask you to excuse us. I have some unfinished business with Miz Shelton. In fact, I think it might be a good idea if you rescheduled your visit to another day." *Oh, crap.*

Parsons' toothy smile disappeared and she prepared for the worst. "I'm not sure I want to do that, Malone. What kind of game are you playing here, Miss Shelton? If you had an interested buyer, you should have told me before I made the hour drive."

"But…"

"Whoa, kemo sabe. I'd watch my tone with Miz Shelton if I were you or I'll kick your ass back to Middleton and save you the gas."

*Double crap.* Things were going south, but before she could intervene, Parsons dug in his heels and took a final shot. "Our first mistake was letting you savages off the reservation."

Oh, hell no. Stepping between them, she got in Parson's face. "Now you listen to me, you bigoted, poor excuse for a human being. I wouldn't list this place with you if you were the last realtor on earth. You've got exactly ten seconds to get your capped teeth and touchy-feely mitts off my property before I use my God-given right as a Texan and put a load of buckshot in your backside before he kicks it."

Jacked up, ticked off and prepared to swear off men for the rest of her natural life, she watched Parsons run for his car. The sleaze ball was tearing ass down the road when Jace snaked an arm around her and patted her butt. "Honey, you do know the law is a little more complicated than that. You can't just shoot someone because you don't like them, even in Texas."

"Of course I know that but maybe he doesn't. He's from Kansas." Wriggling away, she reclaimed some personal space. "What are you doing here, Jace?"

"Taking what's mine."

So he wasn't there to apologize. Well, fine by her. "If you left something here, then take it."

"Oh, I intend to." He closed the distance between them and scooped her up in his arms. "I made a big mistake Friday night and thanks to you I had a miserable weekend. I think we need to kiss and make up."

She fought him. Sort of. His scent tickled her nose and the solid feel of his chest tickled everything else. "You already have someone in your life, remember? You need to put me down and go peddle your passive-aggressive bull…stuff somewhere else. I'm not a used car you take out for a test drive or kick the tires or whatever it is men do when they're buying a car."

"The only someone in my life is you and we're way past the tire-kicking stage."

They were? "We are?" When they got to the Escalade, he shifted her in his arms and opened the door. "This is kidnapping, you know that, right?"

"Sue me."

"I might just do that. Where are you taking me?"

"Back to my place."

"Why?"

"Because the first time I bury myself in you, it's going to be in my bed under my roof, not Gus's."

Okay, maybe one more man and then she was done. Stupidly, she said the first thing that popped into her head. "Gus is dead, Jace."

"Yeah, I know. I just heard him turning over in his grave."

# Chapter 12

He wanted to hit something, and if his little crusader hadn't run him off, Parsons would have been his first choice.

For a beautiful woman, she looked like hell, and he had no one to blame but himself. Thanks to his infernal pigheadedness, the evidence pointed to a weekend spent mostly in tears. Pale as a ghost, her dark circles were more pronounced, and he'd bet the ranch she hadn't eaten a bite. As tempting as it was to lay down the law about her health, he kept his trap shut. From here on out, her well-being was his responsibility, but there'd be time enough to cover all that later. After he got her naked.

He put the Escalade in gear, made a circle in front of the house and took off down the private road. Damn, she smelled good. Whatever she was wearing was subtle and intoxicating, peaches and something he couldn't quite place, vanilla maybe. Eyes forward, hands tangled in her lap, she wasn't going to make this easy on him, and in her place he wouldn't either. Snagging one of her hands, he brought it to his lips and pressed a kiss into her palm. "I see I'm still in the doghouse."

Refusing to look his way, she didn't pull her hand away, a baby step that felt more like a giant leap. "You've been temporarily replaced by that awful Frank Parsons. What he said to you was despicable. Does it happen often?"

"Occasionally, but I try not to let it bother me. I can't remember the last time I shot someone over it."

"It's disgusting. What makes people like that?"

"Ignorance, stupidity, you name it."

"I don't want to name it. I don't even want to be on the same planet with it. How was it for your folks when they came here?"

"It was rough on them at first, but they had each other."

"And you."

"I was more of a problem than a comfort. I was sixteen and mad at the world, my folks in particular. I didn't much like being uprooted from the reservation and my homies."

He moved her hand to his thigh and held it captive with his own. The heat from her hand travelled straight to his dick, a sure sign he'd be lucky to last through the foreplay; but come hell or high water he was determined to take his time with her, gentle her and gain her trust before he claimed her. The taming would come when he broached the subject of DD. If her knowledge was gleaned solely from the Internet, she was in for a rude awakening. Maybe he was too. For all he knew, her feelings didn't extend beyond lust. Even a blind man could see she was turned on Friday night, but that was a far cry from love.

"I can't believe you had homies."

"Oh, hell yeah, real hoodlums. I got it in my head I had to compensate for my Dad being a cop, I guess. We were all headed for serious trouble, and I was the worst, cocky and arrogant as they come."

"Wow. Shocker."

Finally, a smile. It wasn't much of one but he'd take what he could get. "You mind your manners, little girl, or when I get you home you'll feel my belt on your butt before you feel anything else."

"Such as?"

"My mouth on your pussy for starters."

He couldn't have written a better reaction. Her eyes went round as saucers and her tongue came out to moisten her lips. On second thought, he owed Frank Parsons big-time. If it weren't for him, their first encounter after Friday night's meltdown might have been a disaster. Thanks to that good ol' boy, his woman had some other poor fool on whom to focus her anger. He'd talk about anything she wanted, at least until he got her home.

"So you were a bad boy. Is that why your folks moved here, to get you out of that environment?"

"Partly, but Dad wanted Mom out of it too. By the time they moved here, she'd lived his life with him on the res for seventeen years. I never heard her complain, not once, but it wasn't always easy on her. It wasn't a cakewalk for her here in the beginning either. There was a lot of whispering behind her back. What was a pretty white woman doing with a fresh off the reservation *injun?* I don't think she was so much hurt by it as she didn't understand the whole concept of prejudice. Dad used to kid her about being colorblind."

"What happened to turn the townsfolk around?"

"Gus happened. We were here about a month when he was in town picking up supplies and ran into my folks. He noticed people weren't being very neighborly so he decided to do an end-run around the problem. He put the word out that he was having a barbecue at his place the following Sunday and the whole town was invited. I've since learned that was Gusspeak for 'show up or else'.

"Dad put his foot down and said we weren't going. That was usually the final word but Mom took him aside and whispered something in his ear. I found out later she told him they couldn't very well criticize folks for their bias when they were carrying their own.

"By the time we got there, close to a hundred people were milling around. When Gus saw us walking up, he broke away from the group he was talking to and escorted us in. And then he did something I'll never forget. He shot off a couple of rounds from his revolver, got everyone's attention and announced the party was in our honor, a way to welcome his new friends and neighbors. It got so quiet you could have heard a pin drop and then one by one people starting coming up and introducing themselves."

"I wish I'd seen that."

"You were there but you had other things on your mind. The first time I laid eyes on you, you couldn't have been more than four or five, and you were a handful. All the other little girls were in their Sunday best and you were a mess. You'd been chasing frogs in that scuzzy old pond. You walked up to Gus covered from head to toe in mud with this little bitty frog cupped in your hands, and he looked at you like you were the sun, the moon and the stars and you'd just presented him with a bucket of gold. He didn't miss a beat. He put the frog in a paper cup, turned the garden hose on you, and you giggled through the whole thing. Ten minutes later, you were back in the pond and Gus just grinned. You were something, honey."

"I was something all right. I'm sure there were more than a few people who went home that night swearing off having kids."

"Not me. I want kids, a whole mess of them." He pulled the Escalade in front of the porch and turned off the ignition. It was now or never. "I want them with you."

She was fast. Before he could stop her, she'd slipped the notch on the seatbelt and was out of the car. "How damn dumb do you think I am? You don't know what you want. I practically threw myself at you and you handed me my clothes." Waving her arms like a crazy woman, she stomped away from him, stopped and turned around. "I can't do this."

"Now, baby…"

"Don't you dare *now baby* me, Malone. I'm not that fearless little girl who chased frogs. I got bigger and so did my dreams but that's all they are, dreams and fantasies."

*What the hell?* "Just talk to me, okay? I'll settle for that."

"I don't want to talk, and I sure as hell don't want to spend the afternoon between the sheets with you so you can scratch your itch and show me the door."

Sweet Jesus. If she had half that passion in bed, he'd die a happy man— but first he had to get her there. "I hurt you. I get it."

"You didn't hurt me, Jace. I hurt me. I saw you through the window of the café and fell in love. That's messed up. You were right about me. I was on the computer all afternoon. I read everything I could find about you and…the things you write about. I've wanted those things all my life and there you were."

Had he heard what he thought he heard? She'd put it all out there, every goddamn word he'd dreamed of hearing from those luscious lips. If he blew it this time, he'd eat his gun. "Is that it? Because I've got you beat by a country mile. I'm pretty sure I fell in love with a photograph."

"What are you talking about?"

"Six months or so before Gus passed, you sent him some photos of yourself in front of a Mayan temple in Belize. I don't know who took the pictures, but I guess you'd call them candid shots. You were mugging for the camera in one, crossing your eyes and sticking out your tongue. It was the other one that damn near gave me a heart attack. Someone must have said something funny because I could almost hear you giggling. I was looking at a grown up version of a little girl who made a surly, full-of-himself teenager smile for the first time in months. Twenty-three years later, I felt the same way when I walked out of Clay's store and saw you standing there."

"If that's true, why did you push me away?"

"The same reason you're standing there instead of walking into my arms. Fear. I even went so far as to blame my ex-wife and the baggage from our marriage. Five seconds after you walked out on me, I realized I was using that as an excuse. Before you came back to town, having an aroused woman in my bed might have been enough, but not now, not with you. I want all or nothing, the love, the lifestyle and the fireworks. You said it once. Now I want to hear it nice and slow. What do you want, Sabrina?"

# Chapter 13

*Holy Sam Huston.* Over the course of the weekend, she'd laced into him a hundred times in absentia and not once did her tirade include spilling her guts. In the heat of the moment, she'd blurted everything out, but that wasn't embarrassing enough. He wanted her to repeat it. Slowly.

Gone was the nice chatty guy from the car. This was a prime Alpha male with enough testosterone for ten men, maybe twenty. He lifted her chin, forcing her to meet his eyes. "As much as I want to take you inside and have you six ways to Sunday, this goes no further until you spell it out for me, and I mean all of it, including those dreams and fantasies. I'm not playing around here, and you can forget everything you read on-line. I'm prepared to lay out the rules, but I have to hear from you first. I'll tell you this much. I'm not your daddy. I won't make you stand in the corner or write a thousand times *I'll be a good girl.* You're a grown woman, which is what I want in my bed and my home. I won't use a hairbrush on you or a wooden spoon or any of those other things you've read about either. I'll use my hand and my belt and it'll hurt like hell."

If that was supposed to be a sales pitch, it needed work, but if his intent was to scare the bejeezus out of her, he'd done a bang-up job. She was still waiting for the cherishing part when he took her hand. For a second, she thought he was going to lead her into the house, but instead he tucked his car keys in her palm. "I'll be working in my study. Take all the time you want, but if you can't be honest about your needs and trust that I'll never hurt you, then we have nothing further to discuss. You can drive yourself home and leave the keys in the ignition. I won't bother you again."

He could work after that speech? She could barely remember her name. He'd just given her an ultimatum, the result of which would change both their lives and walked away. Who did that? And what was with the who's-your-daddy' speech? Age-play might be right for some people. It was fun to read about, but if he ever tried dressing her in jammies, she'd geld him.

A few drops of rain landed on her shoulders and she looked up, excited to see big fat thunderclouds moving in. She loved rain, always had. She loved running in it, camping in it, even singing in it. Taking shelter on the porch or in the Escalade would be the sensible and smart thing to do, but Lord knows no one would ever accuse her of being sensible or smart. Nope, not her. She'd let the object of her obsession drag her into the car and bring her back to the scene of the crime, and just like Friday night, she was confused, teary-eyed and dripping like a faucet. If Einstein was right and the definition of insanity was doing the same things over and over and expecting different results, she was in need of some serious therapy.

Closing her eyes, she inhaled the bite of ozone and twirled around, her face tilted to the sky. She was procrastinating, another thing she did with annoying regularity. Especially big decisions, and this one was off the charts. He'd tossed the ball in her court. The question now was what to do with it. They'd only known one another three days, technically a few hours, and he loved her and wanted babies with her? She loved him too but…*Jeez Louise*. Things moved fast in romance novels but that was fiction. This was real life, a version of it anyway. When it was just a crazy pipedream, the idea of giving up travel and her independence didn't sound half bad, but could she do that? Maybe she needed to sleep on it. Yep, that's what she'd do. This was too important to let her raging hormones or overactive imagination drive the bus.

"What the hell do you think you're doing?"

Apparently thunderstorms weren't confined to the sky. Hands fisted at his sides, Malone was on the porch looking mad enough to bite the head off a baby chicken. Not that he would. She hoped. "I'm thinking."

In full-out dominant mode, he strode toward her and pitched her over his shoulder. "You're done thinking. From now on, I'm making the decisions."

She squirmed, trying to wiggle free but he shut that down with a way too hard slap on her rain-soaked butt. "Ouch! I didn't agree to anything and you're not my daddy, remember?"

"Yeah, well, I said that before I realized you don't have the brains God gave a goat. You don't need a man, you need a keeper, and I just signed on. I'm putting you in a hot bath, getting some real food into you and then you're going to talk to me if I have to hog-tie you. If you behave yourself through all that, I'm taking you to bed."

"And if I don't?"

"Trust me, you're not going to like it."

# Chapter 14

"Achoo."

"Now see what you've done?" After easing her off his shoulder to perch her at the edge of the tub, he turned on the hot water full blast. "The temperature outside dropped twenty degrees in five minutes and you were out there playing in the rain."

"I sneezed. I didn't cough up a kidney." She batted at the steam filling the bathroom. "You going to bathe me or cook me?"

He was grinning like a fool but accepting that he was going to bathe her was more than he dared hope for. "You probably have a fever too. Let me feel your forehead."

"Quit fussing, Jace. I'm fine."

"You slap my hand away one more time and things could turn ugly. You're a little warm. I think I have a thermometer around here."

She huffed and crossed her arms. "You're not taking my temperature."

Rummaging through the medicine cabinet, he found what he was looking for. Even better, he found a second thermometer his cousin left behind when she visited with her baby. To make his point, he grabbed a jar of petroleum jelly from the shelf, turned around and held the items out to her. "We can do this the easy way or the hard way."

"You wouldn't dare."

"You ought to know me better than that. Besides, this is nothing compared to what I plan to slide into that perfect little bottom of yours."

Part embarrassment, part righteous indignation, her expression was priceless. "We'll see about that. I'll take the oral one. You do know they make digital ones that go in the ear, right?"

"We're kind of old school around here."

He cut off her sassy remark by slipping the thermometer under her tongue. For the next few minutes, he could stand there and stare at her, something he'd never tire of doing. Without a doubt, she was the most irritating, thoroughly unpredictable, amazing creature he'd ever come across, and that was saying something. When he looked out the window and saw her spinning around in the rain, his cock damn near broke the zipper on his jeans.

A few months shy of forty, he'd finally found everything he wanted in one woman, but that knowledge was a double-edged sword, one which could easily rip out his guts. Before the night was over, she could walk out of his life, this time for good. The deal wasn't sealed, not by a long shot. Agreeing to the lifestyle wasn't good enough. She had to embrace it. As much as he loved her, a conventional relationship was anathema to him.

He'd seen too many good people end up in bad marriages because women treated their men like kids and the men had it coming. Chivalry didn't just die. It was assassinated by the very people who should have fought to the death to maintain their place in the grand scheme of things. Men had relinquished their role as head of household and the women stepped in, to the detriment of all. Exhausted from working all day and keeping things together, the woman became overwrought and surly, while the man retreated to his man-cave with his sixty-inch TV and video games or his workshop where he tinkered with cars he'd never drive. Both sides resented the other, and when resentment crept in one door, love went out the other.

Despite what the world at large thought of a man who held the reins and disciplined his woman, it wasn't about ego. The last thing he wanted was a doormat, some submissive little thing who didn't know her own mind, who'd jump through hoops and roll over on command. And it wasn't about knowing her place. His woman's place was beside him, hand in hand facing the problems, exchanging ideas and finding solutions. It wasn't about control either. It was about finding a balance and keeping the peace. A woman who had a strong man to fall back on, one who would tan her hide and not hold a grudge or accumulate baggage, who would respect her and love the stuffing out of her and keep her happy in bed, was a woman who went through the day with a song on her lips instead of a snarl.

The lifestyle wasn't for everyone and Sabrina would be a challenge. Shuffled off to private schools, she was used to living on her own, travelling whenever and wherever the mood or assignment took her. Paris one day, Moscow the next, not a bad life. Would she give it up for a life with him in *Podunk Central*?

"Yes!"

"What did you say?" Yanked back to planet earth, he thought he might be hearing things, wishful thinking at best. Waving the thermometer in front of him, she was all smiles. "I'm normal. See?"

"Honey, the day you're normal is the day I put on a tutu and execute a soubresaut across the room."

Her eyebrows shot up into a fringe of golden bangs. "You learn that in Special Forces, tough guy? I'd pay good money to see you leap across the room."

"I like the ballet. It's disciplined."

"Quelle surprise."

"I know some French too, so unless you want me to surprise you over my knee, we need to get you out of those clothes and into the tub. Stand up."

"I can bathe myself."

He should have seen it coming. She was testing him. He'd wasted precious moments standing there thinking while she was regrouping, finding a million reasons to run from what she wanted. Not happening, not while he had a breath left in him. "You know I'm not going to stand for your foolishness, Sabrina. Are you sure this is the way you want to play this?" When she didn't answer, he snicked the buckle on his belt and drew it through the loops.

Alternating her glance between his face and belt, she had the deer in the headlights look. He'd never cared for that look on other women, but on her it was pure perfection. "What are you doing?"

"Giving you what you want."

"I don't know what I want."

"Sure you do. You just need reminding. Now take off every last stitch, go in our room and lay face-down on the bed. Put the pillows under your hips. I'm going downstairs to take something out of the freezer for dinner, and when I come back I want to see your butt high and your hands gripping the headboard. You might want to remember that position. I have a feeling it's not going to be the last time you're in it."

# Chapter 15

*Be careful what you wish for.* No shit, Sherlock.

She couldn't just take off her clothes and let him bathe her. That was way too smart and sensible. She took the dumb and dumber route. Now she still had to strip, but instead of soaking in a nice hot bath, she was going to get her ass striped with his nasty old belt.

Another sneeze almost knocked her off her feet. Great. If the punishment didn't kill her, she'd probably die of pneumonia. Peeling off her clothes, she bundled them in her arms and looked around the bedroom for somewhere to put them that wouldn't leave water rings. It was a beautiful room, masculine and comfy. Proportionately, this room and the luxurious en suite bath were twice the size of other rooms she'd spied throughout the house. The furniture was massive. Executed in rich, dark wood with elaborate carving, it was something she might have purchased if she ever had a room large enough to accommodate it. Even the colors in the bedding and draperies were her favorites, jewel tones of hunter green, cobalt blue and amber.

Wait. *Our* room? They hadn't even had *the talk* yet and in his mind they were a foregone conclusion. Well, duh. She was standing naked a foot away from his bed ready to submit to a session with his belt. What other conclusion could he infer? Who was she kidding? She wanted this, wanted him and everything he was offering. Just the sound of his voice gave her goose bumps.

Heavy footfalls on the stairs made her heart race, and she scrambled to ditch the clothing and get into position. She was grabbing the spines of the headboard when she heard the door open and close.

"Very nice."

If she'd been capable of breathing, she would have puffed out a sigh of relief. She didn't know what to do with her eyes. Her only experience with punishment was at a fetish club where eye contact was a matter of protocol left to the discretion of the Dom. Preferring to err on the side of caution, she kept them averted and stared straight ahead.

"Do you know why you're being punished?"

"Because I don't have the brains God gave a goat?"

She distinctly heard a chuckle before his tone turned serious. "Let's try that again, shall we? Why are you being punished?"

"I was being difficult and didn't...obey you."

"You hesitated on the word *obey*. You know what I demand in a relationship. Will that be a problem?"

A scene flashed before her. A rally. Her feminist friends were preparing to burn her in effigy, and she was holding the match. "Probably at first, but I'll work on it, sir."

"We'll work on it together, but drop the *sir*. I'm not your Master and you're not in a fetish club. Those days are over. Whatever your needs are, I'm more than willing and capable of meeting them."

That little tidbit skittered down her spine and made a beeline for her clit. They may not be in a BDSM club, but Jace Malone was no slouch in the dominant department. Thirty seconds in his presence and her girlie parts became a flood zone, a fact she was determined to conceal.

"Unclench your muscles and spread your legs."

"Excuse me?" High and squeaky, her voice sounded like she'd just inhaled helium.

The mattress dipped and she turned her head to find him seated near her ass which, thanks to the pillows, was on prominent display. His eyes fixed firmly on hers, he was naked to the waist, his broad shoulders and ripped torso resembling sculpted stone, an artist's perception of male beauty at its best. "This was your choice, not mine. Now spread your legs."

In no position to argue, she screwed her eyes closed and spread her legs.

"Sweet Jesus, you're bare. And wet." Captain Obvious followed his observation by sliding an exploratory finger through her slippery, waxed folds. "And tight. Now that's a shame. I was only going to give you five, but I'm afraid I'm going to have to double it. The punishment should fit the crime and having to whip your ass instead of enjoying this little slice of heaven is a capital offense."

From her perspective, he seemed to be enjoying it just fine. He knew exactly what he was doing to her and was loving every sadistic minute of it. With each stroke of his finger, heat and need made her gush. Clearly sex wasn't a glitch. That was the good news. The bad news was she really wanted to come. She'd never been a screamer, more of a moaner, so maybe she could pull it off without him knowing.

"You know, Sabrina, my dad said something once I'll never forget. He said, 'Son, a man who can't tell when a woman is coming shouldn't be allowed to procreate.' He was referring to women who faked their orgasms but the same thing applies to little brats who get it in their heads to pull a fast one. I'd think twice if I were you."

The threat was implied but potent. He was already going to use his freaking belt on her. What else could he do? *Uh oh.* For starters, he could dip his finger in her juices and trail it up her backside to her anus, her Achilles heel. He probed, just a tiny bit but that was enough. Any further and she'd go off like a rocket. "Wha…what are you doing?"

"Inspecting what's mine. You like that?"

If he knew what was in her nightstand drawer, he'd realize just how much she liked it. She'd been using butt plugs for years as part of her personal playtime routine. "Umm."

"I'll take that as a yes. I'm guessing you've never taken a man up here."

Incapable of forming a coherent thought, she shook her head. Marc had wanted to, but she always found some excuse to put it off. He'd been a victim of her cowardice in more ways than one and nothing would excuse the callous way she'd ended things, or didn't end them as the case may be.

His finger probed deeper, his thumb strummed her clit and that was all she wrote. Writhing beneath his hand, she did a tad more than moan. She shouted out his name. To his credit, he let her ride it out until, sated and embarrassed, she rolled to her side and prayed for death.

Looking none too happy, he got to his feet and crossed his arms. "Are you finished?"

Holy Moly, in that stance his biceps were the size of her thighs. She bet those puppies could wield a belt that would rip her backside to shreds. She was dead meat. As her post-climactic glow gave way to anger, she sprang to her knees. "Now who's playing games? You set me up."

Not a muscle moving in his face, this was pure pissed-off warrior ready to do battle. "I wanted you to concentrate on your punishment and not on staving off an orgasm. Time's up, Sabrina. Where you're concerned, I'm not a patient man. I need you to spell out exactly what you want. But know this. You'd better be real sure you make the right decision. I won't stand for equivocation. If you decide to stay, you're not running back to Gus's or Boston or Timbuktu. This is for life, marriage, kids, the whole nine yards. I'll love you, fuck you blind and spank your sweet ass when you need it and even when you don't. You'll never want for a thing, but if you're just looking for a lover for the next month while you figure out what you want to do with the rest of your life, I'll drive you home right now."

The room spun. Unsure if the vertigo was caused by too much emotion or too little food, she inched toward him on her knees. "Jace, do you love me?"

He took a step forward and cupped her face in his hands. "I love you like the sun, the moon and the stars, baby."

"Good, because I love you too but…" Cold one instant, hot the next, she swallowed a boulder-sized lump in her throat. "I think we're going to have to postpone the punishment."

"Give me one good reason why."

"Okay."

# Chapter 16

She'd be the death of him for sure. The best he could hope for was a few good years before she pulled some damn fool stunt and he dropped dead of a heart attack. During his years in the military and law enforcement, he'd been up close and personal with bombs, bullets, knives and terrorists, but until she fainted dead away in his arms, he'd never known real fear.

That she came to almost immediately gave him some comfort. It was her compliance that worried him sick. Sabrina didn't do compliant. He'd expected her to fight him every step of the way, but she just looked up at him with those big beautiful eyes while he pulled a t-shirt over her head, slipped her beneath the covers and called the doc.

He needed a drink, something to take the edge off while Jeff was upstairs examining her. Uncapping the decanter, the smell of whiskey made him gag.

"It works better if you drink it instead of looking at it. And while you're at it, you can pour me one." Jeff Coleman dropped his medical bag inside the study door and folded his lanky frame into a leather wingback. "I always loved this room. I keep telling Karen we should turn Mike's old room into a study, but she insists his marriage isn't going to work out and he'll be back. She's been saying that for five years."

Opting out of one for himself, Jace poured a good measure of whiskey into a tumbler, handed it off and took the matching chair. "This is my fault. I was putting too much pressure on her. She was playing in the rain, for God's sakes, a grown woman. I should have insisted on getting her into a hot tub instead of lecturing her. She felt clammy when I touched her face but I just thought…"

Before the tumbler reached his lips, the doc grinned and shook his head. "This is a first, Jace Malone a blithering idiot. Of course she was playing in the rain. That's Sabrina. I opened my practice here the year her parents died, so I've been tending to her on and off for twenty-seven years. Who do you think patched her up when she tried jumping old man Johnson's pick-up on her Harley? Evel Knievel she ain't."

"Give it to me straight, Jeff. How sick is she? Should she be in the hospital?"

"She's not sick. Everything checks out fine, blood pressure, temp. I drew some blood but I'm pretty sure we'll find out she's just plain rundown and dehydrated. She needs to start eating better and getting more rest. She couldn't tell me the last time she had a good night's sleep. Just to be on the safe side, I'm going to recommend she get a B-12 shot every day for the next two weeks. After that, we'll see. I can stop by and give it to her or you can do it."

Relieved beyond measure, he took his first good breath in almost an hour. "I'll do it. No problem."

"That's what you think. It goes in her hip, and I don't envy you that. She hates needles. She'd scream like a banshee when Gus brought her in for vaccinations."

"I've got ways to keep her quiet."

"Yeah, about that. Go easy on her, nothing too rambunctious. She'll let you know when she's up for it. You sure about this, Jace? She's a little beauty but, goddamn, she's a…"

"Handful? If you've got something to say, Jeff, spit it out."

"Okay, I will. I've known you a lot of years and been pleased to call you a friend. I've played poker with you, followed your careers and read your books, but aside from your brief foray into matrimony, I've never heard you mention a woman and now I find Sabrina in your bed. She's not the settling down type. I hope you know what you're doing."

"I'm pushing forty. I think I know my own mind."

"It's not your mind I'm worried about. I'm pushing sixty and women still confuse the hell out of me, especially the one upstairs. I'm not convinced a wild child like her can be tamed."

"Watch me."

"I'll do that, and in the meantime I'll phone in a prescription for the B-12 and whatever else I think you need and have them delivered out here in an hour or so. Get some food into her, plenty of fluids and give her an injection tonight. It's important the regimen be followed."

"I love her, Jeff. I'll see she gets what she needs."

"You do realize the two of you are going to be big news, one likely to cause a shit-storm."

"Does that include you?"

"Not me. I'd like nothing better than to see two people I care about find one another and make it work. I'll be pulling for you."

Movement inside the room startled them both. Swamped by one of his jackets as she leaned against the doorjamb for support, his *wild child* looked weak as a kitten and guilty as sin—and then it all went to hell in a handbasket. "Doc, will you drive me home?"

*Compliant my ass.* He should have figured she'd try some asinine move like this. It wasn't so much what she said but the fact that she ignored him as if he wasn't in the room. Silently counting to ten, he stayed seated while affecting a nonchalance he didn't come close to feeling. "Honey, if you think I'm letting you out of bed, let alone out of this house…"

"I've changed my mind, Jace. I know that's not what you want to hear and I'm sorry, but you didn't sign on for this. When I get better, we can talk about things again but for now I think I should go to Gus's. I can take care of myself."

Red-rimmed eyes, quivering lower lip. She'd been crying so he knew it wasn't an easy decision on her part—or a good one—but there was no way in hell he'd take it lying down.

Seeing as how she was fixing to turn this into a war of wills, he was equally determined to win the first battle. If she could negotiate the stairs, she could damn well make the short trek across the study. "Get that sassy ass over here." Shuffling from foot to foot, she dropped her head before moving forward and landing in his lap. He drew her close, nuzzling her neck until she melted into him, her tiny shudder of contentment like music to his ears. "Little girl, what you know about love, you could put on the head of a pin. But you're right. It's probably best we had this talk now. If I ever got sick, I wouldn't want you taking care of me."

With a look of genuine horror, she turned on him. "That's a dreadful thing to say. I'd never leave your side. I love you. That hasn't changed." A few beats passed and he swore he saw the flicker of a light bulb above her head. "Oh."

"That's my girl." He brushed her temple with a kiss and rose, her frail body cradled in his arms. "Let's go, brat. I'll put you back to bed and make you some soup. Jeff's sending over everything we need to get you well."

"I hate taking pills."

"Then you're going to love the alternative. You're getting a B-12 shot in the butt every night for two weeks and don't even think about arguing. I still have my handcuffs and I know how to use them."

"Whatever you say." She laid her head on his shoulder and sighed. "You really have handcuffs?"

"Baby, you are twisted, just one of your many charms."

He'd forgotten they had an audience until Jeff cleared his throat. "Not that anyone cares, but I'm going home. Karen thinks my days are boring. Wait till I tell her I just saw hell freeze over."

# Chapter 17

"You're bringing me back to your room? I thought you'd put me in the guest room out of your way."

She'd said the wrong thing *again*. His expression had danger written all over it. "It's *our* room and I want you next to me where I can keep an eye on you, but if you're worried about me groping you in the middle of the night, don't be. You need sleep, not sex."

Swell. She could add frustration to her other list of maladies. "Sure, why not? Every woman wants to hear she's resistible."

"I never said that. I'll go to your place tomorrow and start packing up your stuff, but for tonight you can wear a pair of my boxers."

The hell with that. After tugging the t-shirt over her head, she tossed it to the foot of the bed. "Thanks anyway but I sleep in the nude."

She wished she had her camera when something between disbelief and horror etched his handsome features. "Since when?"

"Since I can remember. According to Gus, we were watching that old Boris Karloff movie, *The Mummy,* and it scared me so badly I went screaming from the room and refused to wear pajamas from then on out. I talked to a shrink about it once, and he said it probably had to do with associating sleep with death and being swaddled in pajamas, something like that. He said not to worry about it. Of course, I was sleeping with him at the time so he had a vested interest in keeping me naked as much as possible."

"You slept with your shrink?"

"He wasn't *my* shrink. Do you think I need one?"

"No, but I may before the night's out. I don't suppose you'd consider wearing a tank top."

"Sorry." Adjusting the sheet and blanket around her waist, she laced her hands behind her head and fell back on the pillows. She had no shame. Zip. Nada. "Come on, Malone, we're both adults, and with you being so disciplined and all, it shouldn't be a problem keeping this a nookie-free zone."

His gaze fell from her face to her breasts. "What I want and what you need are two different things." Bending down, he swept his tongue across one pebbled nipple and brought his lips a hairsbreadth from hers. "I've been playing this game a lot longer than you and I'm better at it." As a parting shot, he pulled the bedding up to her neck. Rat bastard.

"You don't want me."

"You pull that pouting business with me and you'll get more than you bargained for. You're getting a good night's sleep, that's my choice. Whether or not you do it on a roasted bottom is yours. I'm going downstairs to heat up that soup. Maria makes the best beef vegetable you've ever tasted. What?"

She was on thin ice already, but unlike the pajama issue, this one was a deal-breaker. Sitting up, she tucked the sheet and blanket tightly around her breasts and laced her fingers together in her lap. "I appreciate that you're going to so much trouble, but I don't eat meat."

"Excuse me?"

"The greatness of a nation can be judged by the way its animals are treated. Gandhi said that and I agree. I don't eat meat. Period." She felt the ice cracking beneath her but held strong.

"You do realize we own a cattle ranch."

"You own a cattle ranch. I'm the person outside the slaughterhouse holding a picket sign."

"I'll see what else I can come up with. In the meantime, you stay put. If you pass out again and I'm not there to catch you, you might break your neck." He started to add an addendum but slammed his mouth shut, turned on his heel and left the room.

She'd pushed him too far. Judging from the coldness in his eyes, it was obvious he was having second thoughts. Could she blame him? They were different as night and day, strangers, two people thrown together on a fluke.

Sometimes love and physical attraction weren't enough. With the mountains they had to climb, they'd need more than chemistry. They'd need divine intervention. Everything was conspiring against them, fear, her illness and quirks, his intractable decisions. Now more than ever she needed him to treat her as something more than a problem Fate dropped in his lap. She needed reassurance, not soup.

She was also starting to question her life-long fixation with spankings. Many women fantasized about it, some even goading their partners into it, but very few dove headfirst into a relationship based on the tenets of Domestic Discipline. Concepts that were attractive on paper and in theory often lost their appeal in the harsh light of day. If she'd learned anything in the last couple of years, it was that reality was a cold, wet blanket.

He was right about one thing. This wasn't a fetish club where the decision was hers, where submissives held the power and she was free to come and go as she pleased. Here there would be no safe-wording out. As head of household, if he decided she needed a spanking, she was going to get it. He didn't mess around either. Well into Saturday, she was still feeling the effects from Friday night's over-the-knee action. He hit hard and it hurt.

Marriage? There was no equivocation when it came to that. It terrified her. From what she'd seen of her friends, wedded bliss was an oxymoron. Maybe down the road, a long way down the road, she'd consider it, but if he thought he was rushing her into that institution, he could check himself into one.

And last but not least, there were the good people of Serenity to whom she was a pariah with a capital P. They'd never accept her. Small towns held big grudges. It was the nature of things. Even Doc said their pairing up would be met with a shit-storm. For better or worse, this was Jace's home. He had a history here, a ranch and friends. How long would it be before he grew to resent her polarizing presence? Add that to the other hurdles and there was no way love could conquer all. More than likely, it would wither on the vine and die a slow, painful death.

Swiping at her tears, she swung her feet to the floor. She needed to pee, and while she was in there, she might as well take a shower. The alone time would do her good, and with any luck, she'd slip on the soap, break her neck and solve everyone's problem.

# Chapter 18

*You'll know you've found the right woman when you want to strangle her one minute and nail her the next.* If he'd heard that once, he'd heard it a hundred times from his Dad, but until five minutes ago, he didn't get it. Before the minx landed in his life and knocked him on his butt, every woman who'd crossed his path fell into one category or the other, mostly the latter. He got it now. He was screwed and his old man was laughing his ass off.

Jace doused his face with cold water, braced his arms against the pedestal sink and stared into the mirror. It was bizarre enough that father and son, both cops to the core, had fallen for women with an outspoken skepticism of law enforcement. Throw into the equation that those same like-minded women were Ivy League-educated, liberal-leaning vegans and the laws of probability went up in smoke.

*Wild child* was an understatement. Sabrina was a pistol. Just when he thought he had a handle on her, she'd throw him a curve. All wide-eyed innocence one minute and sultry vixen the next, she'd keep him on his toes. Baring her breasts with that femme fatale routine nearly did him in. He'd wanted to spread her out and devour every last luscious inch of her.

So why didn't he? At the time, he told himself he was being noble and her health was paramount, but that was only part of it. The other part was neither noble nor pretty. Jealousy. Another first. He was jealous of some faceless, nameless shrink who'd found her first. When the brat dropped in that factoid, it stuck in his craw. How many men had there been, five, ten? She didn't seem the type to have random sex, but her sojourn into BDSM surprised the shit out of him, so who knows?

Not that he'd been a saint, far from it. Most of his adult life he'd been a player, and it hadn't much mattered who he'd played with. One drunken night of debauchery, a quickie marriage and three hundred days of hell put an end to that. A month ago, if someone had told him he'd be chomping at the bit to settle down with a feisty little anarchist, he'd have laughed in their face—and then he'd have shot them.

He splashed his face again, turned off the water and swore a blue streak. The master bath was right above the powder room, and unless he was hearing things, the shower was running. The soup forgotten on the stove, he took the stairs two at a time and rounded the corner into the bedroom.

# Chapter 19

"For God's sake, Bri, get a grip. You love him and he loves you. Couples have overcome worse obstacles and made a success of it. Look at his parents. What's the big deal?"

The *big deal* was she was standing in the shower talking to herself. Out loud. And to top it all off, she was turning into her least favorite thing in the world, a bimbo.

Reaching for his shampoo, she unscrewed the cap, took a whiff and then another. It was masculine and sexy, just like the man. She could only imagine going to sleep and waking up every day enveloped in his scent and those muscular arms.

"Sabrina Ann Shelton, if you're alive in there, you've got till the count of three to answer me and unlock this door."

Well, if it wasn't Mr. Buzz Kill himself. If she ignored him, maybe he'd get the hint and give her the few minutes she needed to un-jumble her brain. There was a reason bathroom doors had locks. They were places of refuge and the sooner he figured that out the better. What was he going to do, huff and puff and…

The noise was loud, bomb-blast loud. She opened an eye to find the door hanging by one hinge and Jace glaring at her through the thick glass shower wall. "I hope this little misadventure was worth it."

Misadventure? She was taking a shower, not kayaking down the Amazon. Pressed back against the tiled wall, she opened her mouth to rip off a saucy retort but managed only a squeak.

"That's what I thought." Turning off the water with one hand, he grasped her arm with the other and pulled her out of the oversized stall. Apparently unconcerned that she was dripping all over his shiny floor, he sat on the edge of the tub and tipped her over his lap. Like the previous spanking, there was no warm up and it hurt like a son of a gun, but unlike the last time, this one came with a tutorial. "What part of *stay put* did you not understand? Of all the damn fool things you could have done, taking a shower was the dumbest. You could have slipped on the travertine floor and killed yourself. I haven't waited forty years to find you, only to have to bury you the same week. There's one thing I won't tolerate and that's you playing fast and loose with your health and safety, and if I have to, I'll introduce you to maintenance spankings to keep you reminded."

Between her shrieks, the sobbing and wailing, she caught every other word but got the gist. He wasn't pleased.

When he was finished, he brought her back up and snuggled her into his lap. Her ass was on fire. She could barely take the agony of her overheated flesh against his denim-covered thighs, but it felt so good to be held, so right, that her head lolled to his chest as she hiccuped through the last of her tears.

His voice and touch were gentle as he wrapped her in his arms and rocked her. "It's over, baby. You go ahead and cry and then I'll put you to bed."

It felt like every emotion she'd ever experienced was having a party in her head, but the one celebrating the loudest was joy. The man of her dreams loved her enough to call her on her craziness and keep her safe. How amazing was that? "I love you, Jace."

He brushed at a tear with his thumb. "Say that again and I might have to break a hard and fast rule and follow punishment with some good lovin'."

"I love you very much, but…"

Cupping her cheek, he brought her face around until they were almost nose-to-nose. "Honey, I'm not pressuring you. If you're not up to it, we'll wait."

"It's not that." Like it or not, it was moment of truth time. If he wanted honesty, he was going to get it in spades, but she needed to elucidate her thoughts as calmly and with as much dignity as possible and not spill her guts again. And she wasn't doing it nude. Rising, she grabbed a towel and wrapped it around her, tucking the ends above her breasts. When she was able to put a few feet between them and out of his scent zone, she leaned a hip against the countertop. "More than anything,

I want to believe this will work but…why me, Jace? You were married to the perfect woman. You were a cop and she was a prosecutor. Ipso facto, it should have worked. You and I aren't exactly on the same page when it comes to a lot of things. Have you thought this through?"

He quirked an eyebrow. "Is that it?"

"Not exactly. I'm not baiting you for compliments, but let's be real. I've never been a raving beauty, but at least I didn't scare dogs and small children when I walked down the street. Now I'm not so sure I can say that. I caught a glimpse of myself before I stepped in the shower and didn't recognize me. You could have any woman you wanted, so I'll ask you again. Why me?"

"Ah, you're not so bad. Once we get the hump removed from your back and the warts lasered off your nose you'll be able to go out in public again. Is this about Alyssa?"

Was he laughing at her? Because if he was, throwing the nearest breakable object at his head wasn't out of the question. "I don't know, Jace. How many prosecuting, former Beauty Queen ex-wives do you have? Of course it's about her. I saw her photo. She's tall and gorgeous. Everything I'm not."

"You're right. She's everything you're not. She's vain, shallow and she wouldn't know the truth if it bit her on one of her surgically-enhanced body parts."

"O…okay." Not a marriage made in heaven. Got it.

He stood up and closed the gap between them with a single step, pinning her between his body and the countertop. "You and I might not agree on everything, but I'll take passion over apathy any day of the week. We'll have our share of arguments, that's a given, but part of what makes you special is your commitment to your beliefs. I don't have to share them to respect them, and I'll never ask you to change them for me." With a flick of his long slender fingers, the towel fell to the floor and he turned her to face the full-length mirror on the opposite wall. "Let's get this other nonsense out of the way. What do you see?"

Now that she'd gone and opened Pandora's Pity Party Box, she regretted it but it was obvious he wasn't letting it go, so with a deep breath, she studied their reflections in the mirror. What struck her first was the difference in their heights, the top of her head barely grazing his chin. And don't even get her started on his shoulders. Or his face. Or that amazing fall of midnight black hair.

He moved closer, a grin just itching to break through. "Honey, I'm not sure you're getting with the spirit of things here."

Imagine that. They finally agreed on something, but if this exercise was supposed to make her feel better, it was having the opposite effect. He was sex on a pogo-stick while she looked like a sock puppet who'd gone one too many rounds in the dryer. The tears building, she turned her head away. This was so *not* good. A man like him would tolerate a crybaby just so long before he sent her packing. "I don't know what you want me to say, Jace."

"Then let me tell you what I see." Still standing behind her, he forced her to face the mirror and rested his hands on her shoulders. "I see the most beautiful woman I've ever laid eyes on. I see courage, humor and intelligence. I see a woman who's capable of more love than a man deserves, and I see a man who intends to take every last drop and return it ten-fold."

Game. Set. Match Malone. That last part finished her off, but judging from his smoldering expression and ginormous bulge against her lower back, this was the prologue. The epilogue would wait.

# Chapter 20

Dumbass. If he'd been thinking clearly and had a lick of sense, he might have anticipated she'd be a tad insecure. Dealing with his demands and discovering she had some medical issues was enough to make anyone skittish. Add to that the fact that he'd reacted like a jerk, and he was lucky she didn't run for the door. When he heard the shower, he'd imagined the worst, but instead of taking her to bed and loving every doubt from her mind, he'd gone the *caveman* route and taken her over his knee. If there was ever a time for damage control, this was it.

Slowly, so as not to spook her, he moved both hands from her shoulders to palm her breasts. He loved the way they fit his hands, the small pink nipples puckered and proud. Rasping his thumbs over the distended tips, he watched her eyes flutter closed as her head fell back to his chest. "Open your eyes, baby. You'll want to watch this. It's the part where I show you how *resistible* you are." A brilliant smile preceded a giggle and his heart nearly thumped out of his chest. Fifty years or so of that would suit him fine. "Put your foot on the rim of the tub, but don't you dare come."

The tip of her tongue came out to moisten her lips and she did as he asked, opening her pussy to his gaze. As much as it killed him, his needs would have to wait. Short of her passing out again, there was nothing on God's green earth that would keep him from taking his time, staking his claim in the most intimate way possible. But first he wanted her to witness him worshipping her body, indulging the sensations that blazed through him like a hot Texas wind.

Abandoning her breasts, he splayed his hands and feathered them down her tummy. An image imprinted itself on his brain, her belly swollen with life. It was another in a long string of firsts. When he dropped the bombshell earlier about wanting kids, it shocked him as much as it did her. Children weren't something he'd given much thought to and the debacle with Alyssa had pretty much soured him on the subject. Until now.

He placed one hand on her hip and cupped her mound with the other. Her eyes widened and her breath hitched as his middle finger did a slow slippery slide through her slit. Gathering her cream, he found her nub swollen and ready to play. "Is this because of me or the spanking?"

Driven to her toes by his unrelenting attack on her clit, she made a moue with her cupid bow lips. "I'm beginning to think the two are synonymous."

"Smart girl." He would have said more but he was on sensory overload. She beckoned him in ways no female had even come close. Everything about her drew him in, the silky smoothness of her skin, her unique scent of peaches and passion, even the whimpering noises she wasn't aware she was making. Throw in her childlike expressions and he was a goner for sure.

For someone who'd grown up a tomboy, who'd spent the last few years seeing the world and going head-to-head with men in a male-dominated profession, she was all woman. Except when she wasn't, those times when her guard was down and the child emerged. All pouty petulance, it was the bratty little girl who drove him up the wall and shattered every defense he'd spent a lifetime constructing.

He loved the woman with every fiber of his being, but it was the imp who tied him in knots and brought his dominance to the fore. He wanted to love and cherish her, spoil and protect her, and because he was who he was, he wanted to give her long, hard spankings on her round little bottom until, teary and aroused, she crawled into his lap and filled the dark place in his soul. He was a sick puppy, but by some miracle he'd found the love of his life, the one woman in the world who would accept him, match him kink for kink and make him whole.

# Chapter 21

His intensity startled her. Why was he staring at her as if she were some priceless object beyond his reach? She was right there. In his bathroom.

Naked.

"Come on, brat. We're taking this to the bedroom."

She was airborne again. Swept up and scrunched against his chest, she barely had time to squeal her need for air before he sat her on the bed. "Easy, cowboy. Watch the butt." If spankings were going to be a regular thing, and she'd bet her bottom on it, they'd have to up the thread count on the sheets. To her severely tanned hide, these had the feel of sandpaper.

"And stop calling me brat."

"You want to pick a fight now?" Grinning like the cat about to feast on the canary, he yanked off his t-shirt and hitched his hip next to hers on the bed. He moved in close, the familiar scent of spearmint meeting her nose. "Make love, not war. Isn't that what all you tree-hugging, cop-hating, bleeding hearts say?"

Her fingers found a home in his hair, raking it back from his face. "You forgot veggie-eating, and I don't hate cops. I just think their mental acuity should be tested as often as their shooting skills."

"Uh huh."

She trailed her hands down his chest, all those yummy male muscles way too tempting to resist. Intent on leveling the playing field and getting him out of his jeans, her fingers were fumbling with the zipper when he shook his head.

"Put your hands behind your head and keep them there."

"But..."

"I've been a walking hard-on for four days. You touch me now and it's all over."

Obedience had its rewards. His sensuous mouth began a slow exploration of her face, dropping baby kisses on her forehead, cheeks and nose, even her eyelids, everywhere but the place she wanted him the most. The memory of their one and only kiss still lingered in her mind and on her lips. No matter how angry she'd been with him, and over the previous two days she'd been hopping mad, she couldn't forget that kiss. Sadly, the closest he came this time was the tiny mole above her upper lip, with which he seemed to have an unhealthy fascination. Lucky mole.

By the time he got to her neck, his teeth and tongue had joined the party, nipping and licking their way to her breasts. Her super-sensitive nipples felt every tug and sent tendrils of heat to places already inflamed and ready to erupt. She whimpered and wiggled. Begging was next, but before she could get to that, he took her gently by the shoulders.

"On your tummy, baby."

Dizzy with need, she complied without a moment's hesitation and watched as he pulled a large plastic bottle from the nightstand. Without seeing the label she couldn't be sure what it was, but the color and consistency were that of lube. While her views on all things anal were quite libertine, her hiney had a mind of its own. Her butt cheeks clenched reflexively, tightening when she heard his evil chuckle.

"Relax. It's Aloe Vera but don't let me catch you using it on yourself and don't expect me to use it on you often. A whipping is supposed to hurt, but I'll never give you more pain than you can take. That's a promise."

The effects were immediate, a slight tingling and then cooling relief. It was the first time she'd felt his hand on that part of her anatomy when it wasn't raining terror and she gasped. The damn thing was large enough to practically cover both cheeks. It would be almost impossible not to strike the same area twice. No wonder it freaking hurt.

"You sure you don't need another spanking? I'm a big believer in anxiety spankings, very therapeutic, calms you right down."

"So you say." If she had a brain in her head, she'd let that last comment stand and zip it. Stupidity won. "Is there any occasion when you don't believe a spanking is called for?"

"Not many." Turning her over and flanking her hips with his fists, he planted a soft kiss on her navel.

She was dying. Every time his mouth made contact with her skin, she had to fight the urge to come. Talking was good. It kept her from screaming.

"Birthdays are obvious. What about Christmas?"

"The gift that keeps on giving."

"Valentine's Day?"

"Nothing says I love you like a spanking."

When he nipped his way across her tummy to a particularly ticklish spot, her next query came out on a giggle. "Guy Fawkes Day?"

"That too." The silly banter was over. She knew it from the set of his jaw and the way he leveled those hypnotic eyes at hers. "You need discipline in your life, and I'm just the man to mete it out. Besides, the sight of your little body over my lap and your bottom red from my hand makes me hot. If you were smart, you'd run for the hills."

She wasn't going anywhere, not now, not ever. He'd won her heart and the rest of her was happy to be along for the ride. "Then it's a good thing for both of us I'm not too smart, isn't it?"

Rules or no rules, she wanted him inside her more than she wanted to breathe. Placing her hand over the bulge in his jeans, she squeezed gently, enough to let him know she could take whatever he dished out. And then some.

# Chapter 22

That was it for foreplay. He was already past the point of no return when the little minx decided to take matters into her own hands. Standing, he divested himself of his jeans and boxers and took another few seconds to enjoy the view.

Turnabout was fair play as he felt her hot gaze sweep him from stem to stern before zeroing in on his manhood. "Hot damn, I've won the lottery!"

Annoyance was hard to pull off while his cock was twitching and his ego was doing the happy dance. "You're naughty, you know that?"

"Very naughty, and if you don't kiss me pretty soon, I'll prove it by going out and jumping one of your ranch hands."

He was on her in a Texas minute. Friday night's kiss was the closest thing he'd come to a religious experience, one he'd replayed again and again, but it paled when compared with the one they shared now. Like a man possessed, he captured her mouth with two thoughts uppermost in his mind. Conquer and claim. She gave as good as she got, her ardor elevating his lust to near embarrassing heights.

A violent clap of thunder shook the house and she tensed. Ending the kiss, he pulled back to study her face, but where he expected to see fear, he saw a child's look of awe. Her body softened as she outlined his mouth with the tip of her finger. "Divine intervention. Looks like I'm yours."

"You just figure that out?" Leaving a trail of kisses in his wake, he meandered down her body to the juncture of her thighs. She bucked her hips at the first sweep of his tongue and he steadied her, his hands cradling her ass. Still warm from the spanking, her little mewling noises amped up his enjoyment and the fervor with which he lapped at her cream, her scent and taste driving him perilously close to the edge.

He had years to take his time and feast. His goal at the moment was to coax one more climax from her. Crooking two fingers inside her hot channel, he found her G-spot and sucked her clit between his teeth. With the same sinuous movements he'd witnessed before, she came undone, spilling her essence onto his tongue. This time she didn't scream his name. It came from her lips as a prayer.

Tempering his need to plunge balls-deep into all that wet warmth, he heard Jeff's words in his lust-addled mind. If a toe-curling climax didn't qualify as *rambunctious*, what did? The sensible thing to do was let her rest. It wouldn't be the first time he'd taken care of business in the shower, but if he had anything to say about it, it would damn well be his last.

"You going soft on me, cowboy?"

"That'll be the day, but maybe we need to postpone this until you're feeling better."

"You're the boss."

They were still getting to know one another, but he should have suspected something was up when she smiled and acquiesced without a fight. Sure enough, she rolled to her tummy, brought her knees up and wiggled that sexy pink ass at him. A man could only take so much, and with his libido in the red zone, he didn't have a prayer of following through with his good intentions. He'd deal with his guilt later. Sheathing himself in a condom, he gave her bottom a good solid swat before flipping her onto her back. "You're going to pay for this, brat. I hope it's worth it."

"I'll let you know." Breathless, she reached for his cock. "And stop calling me…"

He entered her fast, her creamy channel gripping him like a vice. From the very first thrust, he was thrown into a tailspin. He'd never wanted a woman so much he didn't know up from down. When he tried to go slow and give her time to adjust to his size, she wrapped her legs around his hips and met him stroke for stroke. His arms taking his weight, he bent his head and bathed her nipple before taking it between his teeth.

Her body arched into him, begging for more. "Oh God, Jace, please."

He felt the pull of her oncoming climax and ground his groin against her clit. Matching his pace to hers, his body prepared for release, everything tightening and loosening at once. When they finally came together, it was a mind-blowing convergence of ecstasy and heat.

He'd seen his fair share of women in the throes of passion but none more beautiful than the woman beneath him. Unwilling to break contact, he waited until her tremors subsided and moved off her, taking her with him, his cock still nestled inside her. He brushed a few strands of hair from her face, amazed that someone who looked like her could be insecure. During their life together, they'd make their fair share of memories but the image of her here in their bed with her kiss-swollen lips and flushed cheeks was the one he'd recall with his last dying breath.

"It was worth it, Malone, in case you were wondering."

"I appreciate the testimonial." Kissing the tip of her nose, he pulled free, disposed of the condom and padded to the bathroom for a washcloth. He loved taking care of her, seeing the blush come to her cheeks as he cleaned her private places and patted her dry. "I suppose at this point I should ask if there are any boyfriends or suitors who might show up and challenge me to a duel."

"You're safe. My job wasn't conducive to dating let alone a relationship. I think my longest was three months."

If that was the bastard who planted the seed of insecurity, he was going to find him and beat him to a bloody pulp. "Tell me about him."

She waited until she was snuggled in his arms, but there was no hesitation, no buying-time or beating around the bush; something he appreciated and rarely got from anyone, the cold unvarnished truth. "I was hired by a production company to go on location and photograph behind-the-scenes stuff. Filming on location is a whole different world. Sometimes you're miles from civilization and you're thrown with the same people every hour of every day. Hook-ups are inevitable and when the filming stops, everyone goes back to their lives. A week after we wrapped, I was on my way to Afghanistan."

"Is that regret I hear?"

"Maybe a little but not for the reasons you think." She grazed her fingers down his cheek. "I didn't love him, Jace. Until I saw you across the street talking to Clay, I wasn't sure I was capable of love."

"Baby, you're only twenty-eight. That's a little young to give up on love."

"Spoken like someone who's been around the block a few times. I'm only twenty-seven, by the way."

"Twenty-seven? I really have robbed the cradle. I've got some mileage on me, honey. You sure you want to hitch your wagon to an old pulp-fiction writing rancher?"

"I'm sure, unless Beauty Pageant Barbie comes after me with a gun or an indictment for stealing her man. I read on-line that the two of you are still close. How's that working for you?"

"What you read is what my publicist put out there, which doesn't bear much resemblance to the truth. I don't believe in airing my dirty laundry in public. I've seen her once in two years when I had to go back to Austin to testify at a trial, and that was once too many. The day she signed those divorce papers was the happiest day of my life. Maybe the second happiest."

"Good save, cowboy," she whispered on a yawn, her eyes drifting closed.

Cocooning her in the blankets, he brushed his lips against hers. She'd fought the good fight but now she needed food, fluids and sleep. "We're going to follow Jeff's rules and get you well, baby, so try not to fall off before I get back with some food."

Soft and dreamy, the eyes that opened to smile at him were ones a man could get lost in. "You may as well know I have problems sleeping through the night. I hope I won't keep you awake."

"Something you want to talk about?"

"Just stuff, you know."

The smile she laid on him was as phony as a three dollar bill but he knew not to push. He'd worked enough rape cases to know the nightmares lingered long after the body healed. Guilt too. There was always some jackhole politician, defense attorney or self-righteous putz who tried to blame the victim. That kind of thinking burned his ass. Rape or no rape, he'd see that those responsible paid for what they did to her. He still had contacts in the military, and before going to Gus's he'd put the wheels in motion with a few well-placed phone calls and emails. "Stuff, huh? I'll accept that for now. You think you can behave yourself for a few minutes while I go downstairs and scramble some eggs?"

"I'll be good."

"Honey, you're always good. It's the obedient part we have to work on."

He was gone ten minutes tops, long enough to check his emails, voicemail and prepare a tray. She was sound asleep when he got back. Lying on her stomach with her head cradled in the crook of her elbow, she looked childlike and vulnerable and took his breath away.

After closing the drapes, he started for the door and stopped for one more glance. *I wasn't sure I was capable of love.* God knows he'd had that same thought a time or two, but that was before this little slip of a thing stepped onto Clay's porch and straight into his heart.

# Chapter 23

Awakened by the sound of the shower, Bri burrowed her nose in his pillow. A lifetime ago, she wondered how it would feel waking up enveloped in his scent. Now she knew. It was like being home.

Her feet hit the floor and she threw back the draperies, looking out to a crystal clear morning. She felt better than she had in months. Even the weather was cooperating.

Today marked the end of her forced two-week bed rest, and she intended to make the most of it. A deal was a deal. He was a tough negotiator but she'd used a few tricks of her own and managed to wheedle him down from the four weeks he'd been insisting on. Technically longer than two weeks, sixteen days to be precise, he remained firm that the first two days didn't count. Waking only for food, fluids and bathroom breaks, she'd slept fortyeight hours straight through.

The subsequent few days were touch and go, about what one would expect in a battle of wills between a recalcitrant *brat* and a control freak. He had a ranch to run and a publishing deadline, both of which he neglected in favor of driving her nuts. Determined to hover and bark orders like a drill sergeant, he backed off when she convinced him less was more. Or, as she so delicately put it, "Keep up the Nurse Ratched crap and I'll kill you in your sleep."

Certain her insubordination would earn her a trip over his knee, she breathed a sigh of relief when he laughed. "You win that round, little girl."

They finally relaxed into a routine. During the day, he did his thing, making periodic visits to bring her food and ensure she was behaving herself. When the weather was warm, he gave in to her pleas for fresh air. After slathering her with sunscreen, he carried her out to the pool and settled her into a chaise. She liked being outdoors, but the best part was the slathering. She really loved that.

Evenings were fun. Cuddled together on the sofa in his study, they watched one vintage sci-fi after another, more often than not dissolving into raucous laughter at the stilted dialogue and outrageous plots, to which they were both hopelessly addicted. But if the entertainment was fun, the after show was spectacular. He bathed her, took her to bed and showed her in every way possible what she meant to him.

It wasn't all kittens and lollipops. During one of his trips to Gus's to retrieve her *stuff*, he found her stash of butt plugs and things took an ominous turn. It gave the evil man another weapon in his arsenal, and he was more than a little enthusiastic about employing it. Caught taking a dip in the pool when she assumed he was still in town running errands, she was promptly hauled over his lap where he inserted the pink one, her favorite, the one guaranteed to get her off. Being punishment and not playtime, coming was a no-no. Knowing full well that leaving her alone to her own devices was counter-productive, he sequestered her on the sofa in his study where he could keep an eye on her as he worked. She squirmed, he smirked and a fun afternoon was had by all. Not.

And then there were the spankings. Hating needles as she did, and in spite of her best efforts to cooperate, she developed Tourette's each and every time he came near her with the syringe. After one tantrum too many, he concluded a good hard spanking would numb her butt so she wouldn't feel the sting of the shot. Yeah, like that worked.

They'd done a fair amount of talking too. He spoke freely of his time in Special Forces and law enforcement, describing a few narrow misses. It horrified her to think that an inch either way and he wouldn't be there, feelings she kept to herself. If she let on how much his stories bothered her, he might clam up and that was the last thing she wanted.

When it came to discussing her work, she shared the highlights but none of the lows, particularly the disaster in Afghanistan. Things were too new between them and she couldn't bear it if he blamed her for putting herself at risk, an accusation she'd hurled at the mirror more than once. Besides, it was moot. That part of her life was over. Not quite twenty-eight, she'd been around the world three times which was more than most people could claim at twice her age.

They'd finally had *the talk* but not once had he asked her to give up her career. He'd hinted at it, of course, but ultimately the decision was hers, one she made happily. Travel and accolades were all well and good, but they couldn't compete with the life she wanted and the man she'd found to share it. Of her two passions, she was prepared to give up one for the other but he wouldn't hear of it. Photography was important to her which made it important to him. He maintained there were options, and they'd explore them together, just one of the myriad reasons she loved him more every day.

There were two unresolved issues, both of which she ignored and hoped they'd go away. No such luck. The first was Carly who called every day to check on the *patient*, calls she almost always deferred to Jace. He suggested on several occasions that she invite her friend over for lunch and girl talk, a sweet gesture and a truly bad idea for which she found myriad excuses not to make happen. Sooner or later she'd have to 'fess up about their lifestyle, but not just yet. She was happy for the first time in her life. The last thing she wanted was a well-meaning friend raining on her parade, and with her narrow view of the world, Carly was a monsoon waiting to happen.

The biggie was marriage. He was insistent and she was scared witless. He'd broached the subject several times and she'd always managed to slough it off as a joke, but how much longer she could do that remained to be seen. She loved him madly and lately she'd been thinking it might not be so bad but…

"Penny for your thoughts." Warm arms enfolded her, his erection hard against her back.

Turning from the window, she looped her arms around his neck. Fresh from the shower with a towel tucked around his waist and his damp hair hanging loose to his shoulders, he filled her with a sense of peace she'd never known. "I was thinking about the last two weeks, how much I love you and how grateful I am for getting me well."

"Grateful, huh?" He moved his hands down to cup her butt and squeezed.

"Grateful enough to spend another week in bed?"

"Don't push your luck. I have to get things sorted out at Gus's and get it on the market before I go to Boston and pack up my apartment. It's silly for me to keep paying rent when I'm not living there."

He tipped her chin up. "Honey, we've talked about this. The last thing you have to worry about is money. The ranch is doing well and I just signed a contract for three more books. If you need to worry about something, worry about the fact that I'm pissed as hell you're going to push yourself into a relapse. You've got color back in your cheeks and now you want to wear yourself out again. I'll go with you. We can spend a couple of hours there and you can come back and take a nap."

"You're on a deadline, remember? Give me three hours at Gus's and I'll come home and make you turkey loaf for dinner."

"One hour and you'll use ground sirloin, not turkey."

"Meatloaf. Yuk." She wrinkled her nose, which for some reason almost always made him smile. "Two hours and be grateful I'm not using tofu."

"Marry me, brat. Make an honest man of me." Feathering his lips across her forehead, the words came out of nowhere in that low Texas drawl that never failed to undo her. Only this time they confused her, and not because she wasn't expecting them but because she yearned to hear them—and damn it all, she wasn't ready. Or was she?

She pushed against his chest, snagging the towel as he landed on his back on the bed. Following him down, she straddled his waist and dropped her head to bathe his nipples with her tongue. His groan was all the encouragement she needed. "Live in sin with me. It's much more fun."

"You've got a knack for changing the subject, I'll give you that."

"I do, don't I? Maybe I'll go into politics. I need a new career anyway. I can run on the tree-hugging, veggie-eating, bleeding heart ticket."

"You forgot cop-hating."

"I'm thinking of dropping that from my platform." Moving to her knees beside him, she licked a pearly drop of pre-cum from the head of his cock. "It seems I've developed a taste for cops, one in particular."

His grin was wicked as he laced his hands behind his head. "I'm all yours."

Her past view on giving oral sex was to take it or leave it, but with Jace it was fast becoming an addiction. Swirling her tongue around the head, she did a slow slide down the length and back up again as her hand caressed his sac. Both in length and girth, he was larger than she was accustomed to and she took as much of him as she could. Her salivary glands jumped for joy, their fluids mixing to give him a warm, wet happy place. When she hollowed her cheeks and hummed her enjoyment, he damn near flew off the bed.

"I'm not going to last, baby, and I want to see your face when you come."

Lifting her easily, he positioned her astride him and she eased herself onto his cock, her body welcoming every last glorious inch of him. She rode him slowly, the way she knew he liked it. Fast or slow, she didn't care, as long as she was touching him, connecting to him. No matter how many times they made love, he found new ways to wrap her in bliss.

"You're beautiful, Sabrina."

The timbre of his voice combined with the feel of his hands anywhere and everywhere he could touch skin sent shockwaves of pleasure from the top of her head to the soles of her feet. With every thrust, her walls clutched and tightened around him. At the exact moment he spilled into her and growled his completion, she followed him into the abyss.

# Chapter 24

Letting loose with a string of expletives, Jace slammed down his cell phone and logged off his computer. It was two weeks since he'd put out the feelers about Sabrina's ordeal in Afghanistan and so far not a nibble. The military wheels turned slowly, his head knew that, but his gut told him something else was in play. Avoidance or denial, the result was the same. He was getting the runaround, and if something didn't shake free pretty soon, he was going to start ruffling feathers and go straight to the top bird if need be.

He added a few notes to the ones he'd already made and slipped the legal pad under a stack of files in the credenza. He didn't like hiding things from her, but she'd bust a blood vessel if she found out he was snooping in her life, even if it were for all the right reasons. For a little thing, she could get up a head of steam faster than anyone he'd ever known and, hot damn, she was something when she was riled up. Like when she was in the throes of passion, her whole body glowed. Her cheeks blossomed pink, those aquamarine eyes turned turquoise and he was toast.

Leaning back in his chair, he grinned at the two photos side by side on his desk. Of all the photographs he could have snatched from Gus's, he took the ones of her mugging and giggling in front of the Mayan temple. The lens caught so much more than just her expressions at the moment. It captured her essence, the playful little minx who'd hogtied his heart.

A loner for most of his life, he'd done a fair job of convincing himself that existing was living and financial success could make up for a cold home and bed. With her ready smile and laughter, Sabrina showed him the error of his ways. Even his writing was better, crisper and more focused. The money from his books was all well and good but it was his need to write that drew him to his laptop hour after hour, the compulsion to create. It was the same with a musician or artist. Or a photographer.

He'd been happy as hell when she offered to give up her career to make a home with him, especially since he hadn't been the one to bring it up, but now he had doubts. She wasn't an amateur fiddling around with her daddy's old Nikon. She was a professional who'd cut her teeth in war zones, the mere thought of which caused his stomach to turn. They'd discussed various ways to continue her career and stay close to home, but he knew in his heart she wouldn't be happy taking portrait shots of babies, no matter how cute they were. Unless they were theirs.

They'd figure it out, but in the meantime he wanted to give her something special, something to show how proud he was of her and the extent of his support. Her birthday was a few weeks off and he planned to surprise her by turning one of the guest rooms into a darkroom. Outfitted with the best equipment money could buy, it would be her refuge, a haven where she could escape and work her magic.

He had another surprise for her too. She'd hinted around about him joining her in Boston, but knowing he had a deadline for his next book, stopped short of asking him outright. Deadline or not, he'd be with her when she closed up her apartment and said good-bye to the city she loved. Stepping out of one life and into another was difficult enough, but the prospect of her doing it alone wasn't an option. He looked forward to spending time away with her, meeting her friends and getting a feel for her life before him. During his one and only visit to Boston when he'd been working a case, it was long enough to get an appreciative overview but far too short to sample everything it had to offer. Having a beautiful tour guide on his arm by day and in his bed at night was a trip he couldn't pass up. The trick would be convincing her to put it off until just before her birthday. While they were gone, Clay was on-board to do the renovation and set up the equipment they planned to order the very next day.

Her reluctance to agree to marriage had him stumped but far from discouraged. He'd wear her down eventually or die trying. What he couldn't wrap his head around was her reluctance to acknowledge Carly's daily phone calls. The woman could be a pain in the ass, opinionated and bossy, but their friendship went back years, so what was up with that?

"The door was unlocked. You got any of that good sipping whiskey left?" Slumped in the doorway, Jeff Coleman looked less like a country doctor and more like a man who'd run a marathon and come in dead last.

"You bet." Jace nodded to a chair and chuckled, "I hope the other guy looks worse than you."

"Seven other guys. The Collins kids are all down with chickenpox. I should have listened to my mother and become a plastic surgeon. I could be in a cushy office in Austin doing boob jobs and tummy tucks."

"It's a shame you never met my ex. Right about now those Collins boys would be looking good."

"I'll take your word for it. How are things going around here?"

"Things are going fine. I didn't have to use the handcuffs once." He wasn't sure what tipped him off that this wasn't a social call, but he went with his instincts. "You know, Jeff, there's a reason I've taken so much money of yours over the years. Your poker face needs some work. What's on your mind?"

Pulling what looked like a photograph from his breast pocket, Jeff glanced at it before handing it off. "You ever see that?"

His breath stilled in his chest. If not this exact one, he'd seen one similar. It was Sabrina at thirteen, lying in a hospital bed, her tiny body battered and bandaged from a motorcycle stunt that went terribly awry. "I've seen it. Something I should know?"

The doc shook his head. "I debated coming here, but we men have to stick together. When I passed the gate to Gus's place, I saw Bri on that damn Harley, and I don't just mean riding it. She was tearing up the road like some freaking Hell's Angel. Knowing you, you've laid down the law. I hate to rat her out, but…"

"I appreciate your telling me, Jeff. We'll have a discussion about it when she gets home."

This was serious. Being housebound for two weeks, she probably needed to blow off steam. He got it. What he couldn't sanction was her flat-out disregard for her safety, the one rule he'd spelled out for her more than once, but obviously not well enough. He'd bide his time. If she brought it up, they'd have a heart to heart. If not, then meat loaf wasn't the only thing on the menu tonight. For dessert, his baby girl was getting a good oldfashioned serving of whup-ass.

# Chapter 25

Bri pulled the key from the ignition and dropped her forehead on the steering wheel. She had a death wish. Taking the bike out for a spin without checking the tires was the dumbest thing ever. Maybe the second dumbest. The spill was bad enough but burning her calf on the exhaust pipe was something only a newbie would do and she'd been riding since she was ten.

It was kind of funny actually, less so when she thought of how Jace would react. When it came to her health and safety, the man had no sense of humor at all.

She'd been excited to tell him she finally called Carly and invited her to lunch; but instead of the café, tomorrow they'd be eating at her very own table in her very own home. *Their home.* In reality, the invitation was about more than going public with their relationship. It was a step toward the altar, a leap in putting her fear of the M-word behind her. She should have quit while she was ahead and left the bike in the shed.

It seemed with every positive step forward she backslid into the same self-destructive pattern. She knew what Sam the

Shrink would say. He'd say she was her own worst enemy, a saboteur whose antics tested the patience of a saint. He'd say she set herself up for failure because she feared commitment and would rather leave than be left. He'd say her parents didn't abandon her, they died. She knew exactly what he'd say because those were the last words he shouted as she rolled out of his bed and out of his life.

The same with Marc, except he never shouted. She never gave him a chance. The minute things took a serious turn, she panicked and snuck out like a thief in the night. They were both good men, amazing men who deserved better than a coward who repaid their affection with grief.

Despite the midday heat, she felt a chill. Was she doing it again, setting up scenarios to sabotage her best chance at happiness? Not while she had a breath left in her. Before she lost her nerve, she needed to talk to Jace, confess to what she'd done and face the music. She needed to grow the fuck up.

She took the long way around and let herself in through the back door. Quietly padding to the study, she stopped and leaned against the doorjamb. He was right where she left him, pounding away on his keyboard, a halfsmile on his lips. Some lucky female was probably getting her butt beaten or her pussy plowed, more than likely both. *Shank 'em and spank 'em.* You go, boy.

Their talk could wait. She didn't like disturbing him, especially if he was in the zone. She liked looking at him though. Everything about him thrilled her to her toes, even when he was all growly and snarky. Biting back a sigh, she turned to leave.

"About time you got home. I could sure use a hug." She pivoted in place and his grin froze into a grimace. Pushing back from the desk, he all but flung himself from the chair. "Good God, woman, what have you done?"

Well, for starters, she forgot to clean up. She didn't even put the damn bike away, just left it where it fell, locked up the house and drove home. This time wasn't nearly as bad as when she tried to jump the pick-up, but she was still pretty shaken up. She ached all over and tomorrow she'd be bruised from head to toe.

The man was a master at dishing out punishment. When he picked her up and carried her to one of the wingbacks, she half-expected to be over his lap instead of curled in his arms, but the gentle way he held her and the disappointment on his face hurt worse than any spanking. A loud sob wracked her body and in seconds she was a blubbering, babbling mess. "I took the bike out and forgot to check the tires and lost control and burned my leg and now you're being nice to me and it makes me feel worse."

"Oh, you're going to be punished. In fact, I have something special in mind. But first, we're going to patch you up, get you into a hot tub and down for a nap."

"I don't want a nap. I want to talk this out. I'm not sure you know what you're getting yourself into, Jace. I have a bad track record."

"And you don't think I'm up to the challenge?" He pinched her chin and forced her to look at him. "I'm in for the long haul. Are you?"

"Of course I am." Her head found his shoulder and a fresh wave of tears dampened his t-shirt. He smelled so good and felt so solid, she wanted to stay there forever. "I'll sell the damn bike."

"That was your daddy's Harley, honey. Gus spent months retrofitting it for your size. Are you sure you want to do that?"

"I thought you'd make me get rid of it."

A chuckle rumbled his chest. "This may be a dictatorship, but I like to think of myself as a benevolent despot. I've got an old hog out back I've been thinking of restoring. We'll fix it up, get yours running again and then we'll ride together. What do you say?"

The image of him riding alongside her with his hair blowing free had her dampening more than his t-shirt. "You'll look hot on a hog."

"You're still getting punished." Reaching behind him, he grabbed a brand new DVD from the desk. "I bought you a present, got it online."

She shrieked when she saw what it was. "*Fifty Million Years to Earth?* I can't believe you found it."

Holding it out of her reach, he quirked his lips. "That's what they retitled it for the American release. What was the original British title?"

She gave him *the look*. "*Quatermass and the Pit*. Who do you think you're dealing with here? Are we watching it tonight?"

"One of us is watching it. I'm guessing you'll be cursing me a blue streak."

*I have something special in mind*. Of course he did, and unless she was mistaken, there was a horrid, pink butt plug in her future. Yep, the man was a sadist, but she wouldn't have it any other way.

# Chapter 26

Still grinning from the effects of their marathon tussle, Jace passed up several spots in front of the hardware store and parked the Escalade at the end of the block. The walk would do him good, although Lord knows he'd had enough exercise for one morning.

He might be a sadistic sonofabitch, but he was a happy one. Insisting she sleep with the plug got the reaction he expected and one he hadn't counted on. By the time the sun rose, she was like a wildcat in heat. If there was anything better than waking up with his woman's pouty lips around his dick, he didn't want to know about it, and probably wouldn't survive it anyway. Turned out that was just the warm-up. Rounds two and three were in the shower, and if she hadn't started obsessing over Carly's visit, it was anyone's guess where round four might have happened.

Whistling as he walked through the door of the hardware store, he stopped at the counter where Clay's part-time helper looked up from a copy of *Road & Track*. "Hey, Jace, how they hanging?"

"High and happy, Deke. Clay around? We're supposed to go over some layouts for a darkroom and order the equipment. I told him I'd be here around noon."

"Don't know nothin' about that. He got a phone call half an hour ago and ran out of here like his ass was on fire. Didn't say when he'd be back. He was looking at some catalogs back in his office. Might be what you're here for, might not. You're welcome to take a look."

Settled behind Clay's desk, he was perusing the stack of catalogs put aside for their meeting when his ears pricked up. British accents were scarce as hen's teeth around this part of Texas but this one was distinct— and familiar.

*"Well, I'll be damned. You're Marcus Tanner. My wife loves your movies. What are you doing in Serenity?"*

*"I'm looking for someone. I understand her grandfather owns a ranch near here. Her name is Shelton, Sabrina Shelton."*

*"Sabrina? Why are you looking for her?"*

*"That's between the lady and me."*

What the fuck? The catalogs forgotten, Jace strolled out of the office. When he reached the counter, he stopped and extended his hand. "Jace Malone. I couldn't help but overhear. We're pretty protective of our womenfolk. I'm sure you understand."

"Marcus Tanner." Accepting his hand, the actor gave him the once over.

"Did you say Jace Malone? You're not Jason Malone, the writer."

"That would be me."

"I can't believe this. I had no idea you lived here. I want to option the film rights to *Cold Fury*. The Head of Development for my production company has been trying to contact your agent for weeks."

"That's probably my fault. My agent runs everything by me and I've been a little distracted the last couple of weeks. You should know it's been tried before but my books don't adapt well to the screen."

"It's never been tried by me. The lead's perfect for me and I want to direct it. I'd like you to write the screenplay."

Deke cackled out a laugh. "Sounds like you boys have a lot in common."

Rife with innuendo, the remark ticked Jace off. He threw the older man a withering look that sent him scurrying back to his dog-eared *Road & Track*.

Preoccupied with staring out the front window, Tanner missed the byplay and inclined his head to indicate the café. "As long as I'm here, I'd like to make my pitch. Do you have time for a cup of coffee?"

He had all the time in the world. He couldn't care less about selling the rights to *Cold Fury* or writing a screenplay, but he'd play the game, at least until he found out why megastar Marcus Tanner was sniffing around. "There's a bar down the road. This time of day, it might give us a bit more privacy."

"Great." Tanner beamed his twenty-million-dollar-a-film smile. "And you know where Sabrina is, right?"

“We’ll talk about that too.” *Count on it.*

# Chapter 27

"What the hell?" Bri slammed the antiquated wall phone back in its cradle and plopped into a chair at the table she'd been fretting over for two excruciating hours. Carly never cancelled without calling and she wasn't answering her cell phone, nor was Clay or Tommy. If she'd gone into early labor, surely someone would have called to let her know.

Over-reacting much? There were a hundred reasons why the prego princess could be late, not the least of which was her pathological indifference to anything and everything vehicular—like when you had to put gas in them now and then to make them go. With a sigh, she fiddled with the floral arrangement and was straightening the silverware for the umpteenth time when the doorbell rang. Sprinting through the kitchen and foyer, she threw open the door. "Tommy, Clay, what are you…" Both men wore such stone cold expressions that her hand flew to her mouth. "It's Carly, isn't it? Is she okay?"

"Carly's fine. Where's Jace?" Clay's tone was clipped, so different from his normal easy-going manner it made her flinch.

"He's in town running errands. What's wrong?"

With an awkward half-turn, Tommy acknowledged a woman behind them. "Bri, this is Helen Davidson. She's a counselor at the battered women's shelter in Middleton. Why don't you go up and pack a bag. You can stay with us as long as you need to, but we don't think you should go back to Gus's."

"*You* don't think?" An icy pang of dread replaced the panic of the previous few minutes and she met both men's eyes with ill-concealed fury. "You have exactly thirty seconds to explain those remarks and tell me why a counselor from a battered women's shelter is standing on this porch."

Professional and polished, the fiftyish woman stepped into the breach and smiled. "We're here to help, Sabrina. May I call you Sabrina?"

"It depends on what kind of help you're here to render, *Helen.*"

"Of course, dear. I find honesty is always the best way to start off any new relationship, don't you agree? Your friend Carly Wilkins got in touch with us and asked if I'd come out and talk to you. She was here earlier when you were lying around the pool in your bathing suit, and she saw evidence of abuse, some rather severe bruising."

The ground shifted beneath her, but rather than grab the door frame for support, she braced her legs and squared her shoulders. If she was going down, she was going down swinging. From the corner of her eye, she saw Carly alighting from a car. She addressed her response to the woman, but left little doubt for whose ears it was intended. "You must be mistaken. I don't have any friends who would skulk around my house and go behind my back without talking to me first. Someone I've known all my life would never think so little of me that she'd assume I'd let some man abuse me, no matter how much I loved him."

"Come on and get in the car, Bri. We'll talk it out, okay?" Unfazed by her remarks, Carly continued her approach, her tone oozing patronizing pathos. "After what you went through in Afghanistan and Gus's death and all, I guess I understand how you could wind up under Jace's thumb. He's trying to isolate you from everyone. It's what controlling and abusive men do. When you were sick, I wanted to come and visit but he said…"

"I know what he said, Carly, because I told him what to say to you. He offered several times to make us lunch by the pool but that doesn't fit into your neat little concept of an abusive man, does it? Not that it's any of your business, but I fell off the bike yesterday, which is how I got the bruises. Now I want you all to leave."

"Stop protecting him, Bri, and listen to Helen."

Her head pounded and nausea roiled up from the pit of her stomach. This was all her fault. By wanting to reach out and share her happiness, she'd brought this ugliness to their home and now she had to clean up the mess. "No, you listen. Ever since I can remember, there have been two constants in my life, you and Gus. You and I haven't seen eye to eye on most things, but I loved you and was prepared to cut you some slack for your black and white view of the world. But here's a news flash for you, girlfriend. I thanked God every night I didn't share that view. There are grey areas, Carly, lifestyles and beliefs that don't fit into your narrow-minded scope. I'm in a relationship that works for me, the only one I've ever wanted with the only man I've ever loved.

"And you, Clay. Shame on you. You've been friends with Jace since you were sixteen. Do you really think he's capable of doing what you're suggesting? You have a short memory too, Tommy." She couldn't go there. Although he'd bought into Carly's hysteria, Tommy's DUI was no one's business, nor was the fact that Jace saved his teaching job by having the citation expunged.

Tommy's eyes met hers but only for an instant. Was it regret she saw before he lowered them, refusing to look at her, and did it really matter since the damage was done? "I'm sorry, Bri, but we all thought…"

"You didn't think and that was your first mistake. I'm sorry you were dragged into this, Helen. I know you meant well and I appreciate the work you do. I mean that. It can't be easy doing what you do, and if I ever meet someone who's being abused the way my so-called friends think I am, you'll be my first call."

"You're in a DD relationship, aren't you?"

That was the last thing she expected but there was no censure in the woman's tone, only kindness. "Yes, I am. How did you know?"

"Because I was too, for almost thirty years. I lost my husband last year to MS. Unless someone is wired that way and lucky enough to find the right man, they'll never understand. Take my card. If you're ever in Middleton and have time for lunch, I'd love to talk to you more. Does your man treat you well?"

"Like a bucket of gold."

With Tommy helping her ascend the final step to the porch, Carly was livid. "Are you people insane? You're talking like beating a woman is acceptable behavior. It's deviant."

Before Bri could lash out a retort, Helen cut her off. "Get your facts straight, Ms. Wilkins. No one is condoning a man beating a woman, and unless they've passed a law I don't know about, you don't get to decide for the rest of us what is and is not acceptable behavior. I have a Ph.D. in Psychology and I've testified in at least a hundred trials involving spousal abuse and crimes against women. I've seen the results of deviant behavior far too many times in my fifty-five years, photographs of victims so ugly they turn your stomach."

With a deep breath, she straightened her skirt. "I have my car and can find my way back. Good luck to you, Sabrina."

The four of them watched the woman leave the porch and Carly shook her head. "I don't understand. He gets mad at you and hits you and you let him."

Exhaustion overwhelmed her. She had just enough energy to end this before she crawled into bed and bawled her eyes out. "It's not like that, Carly, but you'll never understand. Jace would never touch me in anger. This drama isn't good for you or your baby. Go home and put your feet up. You all need to leave before he gets back. I don't want him to know about this."

Tommy and Clay were mumbling apologies but it was Carly's voice she heard. "I can't deal with this, Bri."

"I never asked you to deal with it, and I won't. Ever. I don't doubt your motives were pure, however misguided, but I just realized something that hurts even more than this ill-conceived witch-hunt of yours. I didn't lose a friend today. You did."

# Chapter 28

"I don't trust anyone else to write the screenplay, Malone. I'm not sure the world's ready for the Domestic Discipline angle, especially American audiences. Maybe you can change the context to Dominance and Submission. We'll ride the coattails of that trilogy that was popular a few months back."

"Uh huh." They could have been discussing the weather for all the attention Jace was paying to *the pitch*. His mind was elsewhere. He wanted to cut to the chase, go home and find a venue for round four. "Why the sudden interest in doing an action film?"

Tanner shrugged. "I'm bored playing romantic leads opposite dewy-eyed starlets, and I'm too young for the wise old codger roles. The alternative is going back to my theatrical roots at the West End and starving to death in mediocre revivals. I regret to say I've grown accustomed to the money. In case you haven't noticed, even bad action films score big at the box office. If you don't have kids flying around on brooms or horny vampires and werewolves, you'd better have muscle, automatic weapons and explosions."

Contrary to his initial impression, he liked Tanner. He'd like him even better if it weren't for the elephant in the room, a shapely little blond who wore her past close to the vest. It was a stretch to think Tanner came all this way to offer her a job but stranger things happened in tinsel town. She'd worked for a production company once, that location shoot in Belize. A romantic attachment seemed likely but why hadn't she mentioned him? Any other woman would be crowing about bedding a movie star.

"I'd like to wrap this up before the month is out, Jason. At least think about it."

"I'll do that but there's a catch. If we can come to an agreement and I sign on to write the screenplay, I'd insist on doing it from here. I have a ranch to run and some other commitments."

"No problem. You really do own a ranch. I thought that was just something to fill out your bio. I'm impressed. Special Forces, Austin P.D. You're the real deal, aren't you?"

Whatever the hell that meant. "When are you headed back?"

"That depends on Sabrina. How well do you know her?"

Damn good question. "My folks moved to Serenity when I was sixteen and she was four or five. I can't say we stayed in touch, but I was close to her granddad during his final few months. He passed away six months ago."

"Bloody hell. I'm sorry about that. She talked about him all the time. He was a Texas Ranger if I remember correctly, somewhat of a legend around here."

"Next to my own father, Gus was as fine a man as I've ever known."

"That explains why she came back here. Her landlord in Boston wasn't the most talkative bloke I've met."

Tanner wasn't the only actor in the room. It took every bit of his training as an investigator to keep his tone modulated and his demeanor relaxed. "Sounds like you two haven't been in contact for a while."

"I was giving her space, as you Americans are fond of saying."

"How'd you two meet?"

"I was filming on location in Belize, and she was hired to shoot publicity photos. I didn't want to do the bloody film in the first place and after about a day and a half, I was turning into the kind of asshole celebrity I swore I'd never be. Two weeks into filming, a helicopter landed a quarter mile away, and she jumped out with a duffel bag in one hand and her camera equipment in the other. I noticed her, of course, who wouldn't? She was this little dynamo wearing cargo pants, desert boots and a Boston Red Sox baseball cap. One of the A.D.s introduced her and then we went back to work, or tried to. Unfortunately, the scene dragged on for hours and I lost it. I started yelling at everyone and throwing my weight around. People were running for cover, everyone but her. She was standing off on the sidelines with that stupid baseball cap turned around just clicking away, capturing every moment of my tantrum. I was good and pissed, and by the time I got to her I was ready to shove the camera up her ass. You know what she did? She smiled at me and said, 'Mr. Tanner, there's nothing wrong with you that a lot less red meat and a little more fiber in your diet won't cure.' She basically told me I was full of shit and walked away. That was it. I pursued her like a lovesick teenager. I wore her down and we were inseparable for the rest of the shoot, almost three months. The last night before we left, I asked her to marry me. She said she'd think about it while she was in Afghanistan. I begged her not to go and come back to the States with me, but when I woke up the next morning, she was gone. I said 'fuck it' and went on with my life."

"And yet, here you are."

Tanner's eyes narrowed as his mouth formed a mirthless grin. "She's with you, isn't she? Christ, she's only been back a month."

"I won't deny it was fast but when something's right, it's right."

"With Sabrina, the beginning is always fast. It's the ending that's the killer, the months afterward when you lay awake at night trying to figure out what the fuck you did to make her run." He rose and dropped some bills on the table. "Someone from my production company will be in touch with your agent."

"Under the circumstances, I'm not sure that's a good idea."

"Trust me, Malone. By the time the ink's dry on the contract, you'll need someone to commiserate with. It might as well be me."

# Chapter 29

Groggy, Bri reached for the clock on the nightstand. 5:10? She'd slept the afternoon away, hours when she should have been packing and running as far and fast as she could. It's what she always did. When things got messy, she booked it out of town, and if Carly's craziness and the email from her landlord didn't qualify as messy, what the hell did?

That was the old Bri. Sometime during the past two weeks she'd grown a backbone. The naysayers could pound salt. The new, improved version would stay and fight. There was nothing the world could throw at them that they couldn't handle together.

She felt the familiar flutter in her tummy as noise drifted up the stairs from the study. After a quick trip to the bathroom to repair the ravages of her tear-induced coma, she was ready to face her future by coming clean about her past. On the off-chance Marc showed up in Serenity, she didn't want Jace blindsided. She'd gone back and forth about revealing Carly's vigilante visit but decided to go with her first inclination and keep mum. What he didn't know wouldn't hurt him. She was still smarting from it, but like yesterday when she fell off the bike, he'd be there to hug away the hurt.

That was the thing about life. Most days she was an active participant but sometimes she could only observe from the sidelines as things went terribly, terribly wrong. Twenty-four hours ago, she stood where she was standing now, watching him work with a smile on his face. Today he wasn't smiling as he took the photos off his desk and shoved them in a drawer.

On wobbly legs, she took a tentative step into the study. "Why did you do that? You fell in love with me because of those photographs, remember?"

"That was before I found out they were taken by one of your lovers."

"You talked to Marc."

The slamming of the drawer sounded like a gunshot and she jumped. A bullet would have been kinder than his look of disgust. "Yeah, I talked to him, and you might want to warn me the next time you're expecting one of your fuck buddies to show up."

"I didn't know, not for sure anyway. I haven't been online in a couple of days and when I checked my email today, there was one from my landlord in Boston. He said Marc was there over the weekend and he told him I'd come back here. I did try to call you. Before I fell asleep, I tried your cell phone several times but couldn't get through."

"I turned it off when I drove to Middleton to look at some stock. I needed time to think."

*Time to think.* It was too much to hope she was still asleep and this was some horrid karmic nightmare, but she knew better. This was all too real. Whatever went down in town changed everything. "I wasn't in love with him, Jace. Is this about him being a celebrity? You're the last person I'd think of as star struck. Would we even be having this discussion if he were someone behind the scenes?"

"That's not the point and you know it. You lied to me."

"I never lied to you. I told you I was with someone for three months. What difference does it make who it was?"

"I don't have time for this. I'm riding out with a couple of hands to check the fences. Don't wait up." He breezed past her through the door, avoiding even the slightest contact, a brush of skin, a glancing touch.

Desperate to hear something, anything that wouldn't signal the end, she followed him into the foyer. "Do you want me to sleep at Gus's tonight?" *Please, please say no.*

His back stiffened, and when he turned to face her, his expression foretold her greatest fear. "Tanner has your M.O. nailed all right. Cut and run. It's what you do when things get serious, isn't it? Probably a good thing I found out sooner than later. Maybe you should stay at Gus's."

Like a lion on a rampage, his words roared in her ears before devouring her dreams. It was the epilogue she'd been dreading and it brought no happy ending for her. For them.

The breath left her but there were no tears or recriminations. It happened so fast—as if pulling off a Band-Aid, quick and painless. Except it wasn't. It was the strangest thing, the feeling she was made of glass, that a breath too deep or a word too loud would shatter her into a million pieces. "You lied too, Jace. You promised you'd never give me more pain than I can handle, but this pain in my heart, I can't even come close to handling it." Grabbing her tote bag and keys off the hall tree, she cast a final look around the foyer. "You can box up my things and leave them on the porch or burn them. I don't care what you do with them."

# Chapter 30

Long minutes after the Jeep pulled away, he was still staring at the door, his heart beating out of his chest. If he could cut it from his body and present it to her on a platter, he'd gladly go in search of a knife.

His anger had sharpened on the drive to Middleton and back. With every mile of road, the image of her with Tanner screwed with his mind. By the time he got home, he was crazed. The photos were the last fucking straw.

And then she was there. Wrong place, wrong time. Looking all sleepflushed and innocent, she'd never know how close she came to being stripped, bent over his desk and whipped till she bled. In the end, he did something far worse. By unleashing his demons, he betrayed every last oath he'd made to her. *To love and cherish, protect and forgive.*

"What the hell's going on? First Bri damn near runs me off the road and now I find you standing there like some whacked out zombie."

Clay's voice hit him like a spray of cold water. He didn't remember walking into the study or taking the photographs from the drawer. Setting them back on the desk, he cleared his throat. "I didn't hear you come in."

"Is this about what happened earlier?"

He needed aspirin and a strong cup of coffee. What he didn't need was a reprise of the day from hell. "I don't want to talk about Tanner."

"Who's Tanner? When's Bri coming back?"

"Why?"

"Because I came here to eat crow and apologize and I was hoping to only do it once. Fuck it. After I left here today, I went to Gus's. It's not that I didn't believe her when she said she fell off the bike, but I wanted to see for myself. I didn't have to look far. She must have left it where it spun out on her, right in the entrance to Gus's private road. What a goddamn mess. She's lucky she didn't break her neck this time." Cocking his head, Clay scratched the back of his neck. "You don't have a clue what I'm talking about, do you?"

"No." Didn't know. Didn't care. He'd only been half-listening anyway.

"You want some coffee?"

"You got anything stronger?"

"You know where the whiskey is. Bring it in the kitchen." A zombie wasn't a half-bad description. He put his brain in neutral and went through the motions. Pour the water, grind extra beans. If he was going to have his balls handed to him later, he wanted to be awake for it.

After lacing his coffee with a good amount of booze, Clay leaned forward. "Before you start punching, just hear me out, okay? You're not going to like this."

"I don't like it already. Start talking."

He hated every last minute of it. Hearing she'd fought the battle on her own was hard enough, but knowing he'd been the one to rub salt in her wounds was pure torture.

"I should have known better, Jace. I love my sister but it's her way or the highway, always has been. Bri was right about her. She ripped into Tommy and me pretty good too. You're a lucky man. Made me realize all women aren't like my ex. I don't mind admitting I'm envious as hell."

"Don't be. I may have blown it tonight."

"I figured something like that. Can you fix it?"

He had to fix it. Whatever it took. "I'm sure as hell gonna try."

"For what it's worth, I hope you do. I won't pretend to understand this thing you two have going, but Bri said something I've been chewing on all afternoon."

"What was that?"

"I'm in a relationship that works for me, the only one I've ever wanted with the only man I've ever loved."

The sun was down as he pulled the Escalade onto the main road and gave it the gas. He'd driven a half mile or so when the lights from an oncoming vehicle flashed once before the driver pulled to the shoulder. By the time he came to a stop and opened the door, she'd already jumped from the Jeep and was barreling across the narrow two-lane road, laying into him like a preacher in a whorehouse.

"If you've got my things in that big old gas-guzzlin' SUV, you can take them right back. I'm sorry you had a bad day, but so did I, and I'm not letting you kick me out of your life because you're in a snit. I didn't tell you about Marc because I was ashamed of the way I treated him and maybe it's coming back to bite me in the ass but…"

*Snapping blue eyes, bright red cheeks. She was something all right. Hell on wheels.*

"I love you, Jason Malone, and I know you love me too and we're just going to have to work this out. I've made a lot of mistakes but loving you isn't one of them. The townsfolk think I'm a horrible person, but they're going to have to get over it too. We have as much right to live here as they do. I was born here and all our folks are buried here. It's our home, and if the good people of Serenity don't like the way we live our lives, they can damn well move."

His face hurt from holding back a grin. "You finished?"

"No." She poked his chest. "We had a deal and you broke it, and I'm really mad at you. When I screw up, you're supposed to punish me but not push me away. I can't let you do that again. You have to promise me and mean it this time. You still love me, don't you?"

Her eyes pooled with tears and it about did him in. Wrapping her in his arms, he gave a silent prayer of thanks when she encircled his waist and relaxed against him. "Baby, words haven't been invented to describe how much I love you. I was a complete ass and I'm sorry. I'll make you two promises. It'll never happen again. You have my word."

"You're forgiven. What's the second promise?"

"When we get home, I'm going to spank your beautiful bottom and tie you to the bed for a week."

She looked up at him, a pouty frown on her face. "The last part sounds good but what the heck did I do to earn a spanking?"

"I'll think of something. Must be a holiday somewhere."

<h1 style="text-align:center">Chapter 31</h1>

"My Daddy said your firm was the best but I'm beginning to have doubts. You've made a mistake." Alyssa slid the glossy eight-by-ten back across the crisp white tablecloth and reached for her wine glass. "Jace would never take up with someone like that. Look at her."

"I've seen her, ma'am. I took the photographs. That one was taken yesterday outside your ex-husband's home."

"Don't get snippy with me, Mr. Turner." There was something about military men that revved her engine, but good-looking or not, this one was aggravating her. "Who is she?"

"Her name's Sabrina Shelton, twenty-seven, born in Serenity. Her parents died when she was nine months old and she was raised by her paternal grandfather, a Texas Ranger of some repute, now deceased. Malone and he were friends. He gave the eulogy at the old man's funeral."

"That explains it then. He always was a sucker for sob stories. He's probably just looking after Serena. I'll bet the poor thing doesn't even have a job."

"*Sabrina* is a professional photographer, a good one too."

"You mean someone who goes into schools and takes pictures of kids?"

"I mean someone who goes into warzones and captures the action on film. She's been published in several prestigious magazines, most recently in *Time*. She's also won several awards. One article compared her to William Eugene Smith."

"I don't care if they compared her to Daisy Duck. She's not his type at all. Where's she living?"

"Her primary residence is Boston. She flew back to Serenity a month ago to deal with her grandfather's estate. Two weeks later, she moved in with your ex."

"That proves nothing. You find out anything about what else Jace has been up to, besides taking in strays?"

"He had a meeting with Marcus Tanner earlier today. The town was buzzing about it before I left. Something about a screenplay."

"Marcus Tanner?" Visions of red carpet moments danced in her head. "Well, that is something. Sounds like my husband's about to hit the big time."

"There is one more thing. One of my colleagues knew Malone from his days at Gitmo. He found out through the grapevine your ex is making inquiries about an incident in Afghanistan involving Miss Shelton." Pulling several sheets of paper from a slim attaché case, Turner placed them on the table. "Those are copies of emails Malone sent out within the last two weeks. As you can see from the context, he doesn't want her to know he's looking into the incident, so I trust you'll be discreet."

She read them over quickly and smiled. "I do believe you've redeemed yourself. Tell me, Mr. Turner, does discretion work both ways? If so, I think we should finish our drinks and go back to my place where I can thank you properly."

Turner rose from the table and pushed in his chair. "Ma'am, with all due respect, I get paid to do your dirty work but I don't have to fuck you. The only man who's getting lucky tonight is Jason Malone."

# Chapter 32

"You're warm, baby."

Minus the subtitles, the scene was straight out of a Fellini film. *A spill of sunlight through the drapes, air heavy with sex, a naked hunk fondling her ass.* If she were any hotter, she'd combust. Stretched out on her tummy, Sabrina rested her chin on her hands. "Whatcha doing back there, cowboy?"

"Appreciating this fine bit of horseflesh."

"Appreciating it or admiring your handiwork?"

"They're beauties, all right," he said with a chuckle.

Yesterday had pretty much sucked but she wanted to remember the ending, every detail, good and bad. Closing her eyes, she drifted back to the moment she'd spotted his vehicle coming toward her. With the moon and stars as witnesses, they'd put the madness behind them. On the surface, all was well. It was what lay beneath the sweet words and caresses, a feeling of unfinished business between them.

The drive home had been a rollercoaster, her emotions careening from elation to remorse, her propensity for secrets almost their death knell. While an erotic spanking and an hour of frenzied sex would have been nice, the last thing she'd wanted was *nice*. Nice wouldn't cut it. She'd craved dominance and mastery, release from the debilitating numbness of regret.

How he sensed it was mystery, but from the instant they returned to the house, her dark warrior took control, an unyielding port in the storm. "Talk to me."

So she did. Sometime before dawn, she'd wiggled free of his death grip and tiptoed to the bathroom. There, in front of the full-length mirror, she stared at her backside and ten lovely red welts from his belt. Absolution and resolution, a double whammy. So to speak.

Today the slate was clean. The guilt was gone and with it her fears. After last night, there wasn't a doubt in her mind about marriage. If Jace had faith in *happily ever after* for them, could she do less?

As if reading her thoughts, he turned her over and spread her legs, his magnificent cock locked, loaded and ready for action. "I need you again. Now."

Giddy with happiness, she gave in to a giggle. "You're insatiable."

His grin would melt a polar ice cap. "If you think I'm going to let all this wet heat go to waste, you're…"

Everything ground to halt. *The Ride of the Valkyries?* As mood music, Mozart was her preference, Mahler in a pinch, but no way was she fucking to Wagner. "What is that?"

"It's my cell phone. Ignore it."

She tried her best and so did he but it wasn't their finest performance. In lieu of an encore, he sprinted from the bedroom and locked himself in the study. An hour later, showered and dressed, she paced the kitchen, listened for signs of life from the study and wondered how, for the second day in a row, a perfect morning could be devolving into chaos.

When he finally appeared, he looked like death warmed over. Worse, he looked like a man who wanted to be anywhere but there. Not angry exactly, just…detached. "Something smells good. I'm going to grab a quick shower."

Maintaining her composure, she eked out a smile. "Breakfast is in the warming drawer. Take all the time you need."

He took ten minutes, ample time to give herself a pep talk and vow not to ask what was up. If he wanted to tell her, he would.

"I'm driving to Austin this morning. I'm not sure when I'll be back. Two days, maybe three. Will you be all right?" His voice sounded like he'd swallowed ground glass.

"I'm a big girl, Jace. I can take care of myself."

"That'll be the day." He pushed back from the table and tugged her into his lap. "You know that case I told you about, the last one I worked before I left the force?"

"I remember." How could she forget it? It was horrific. A man raped and brutally murdered his two young daughters.

"There's an issue with the chain of custody. The prosecutor thinks the bastard's defense team intends to base their case on improper handling of the evidence. I spent the last hour going over my notes and there's no way."

This was a side of him she'd never seen, the outraged victims' advocate. Her heart ached for him. To work so hard at getting justice for two innocent children and have the rug pulled out from under him had to be devastating. "You said the trial didn't start for six months. Surely you and your partner can sort it out before then."

"At the defense's behest, yesterday the judge moved up the trial date to next month. Mike's on a two-week cruise with his wife. I'm not even sure he knows. I'm on my own."

The more he talked, the more it sounded like a made-for-TV movie. *Embattled ex-cop fights the system to put away a monster.* Still, even embattled ex-cops had to eat. "Do you have time for breakfast?"

"Afraid not. It's almost ten and the D.A. called a meeting for two o'clock. It's at least a three-hour drive and I'd like to do some nosing around before I go under the gun."

She had a million questions, starting with whose ringtone triggered their coitus interruptus on a Saturday morning, but he had enough on his plate without her petty insecurities. Kissing him quickly on the cheek, she slid off his lap. "Then it's time to hit the trail, cowboy. Give 'em hell."

Twice he headed out the door and both times he came back to kiss her socks off. The third time he made it as far as the car, loped back to the porch and gazed up at her. "Just so you know. These last three weeks have been the best of my life. I love you, baby."

Speechless, she watched him climb into the Escalade. It was only after it disappeared down the road that she realized she hadn't responded. They were beautiful words, and it wasn't as if he hadn't said them before, but this time she couldn't shake the feeling of finality. She wasn't a fatalist, far from it, but if the Fates had something in mind for them other *than happily ever after*, they'd have a fight on their hands.

In the meantime, she had better things to do than dwell on accidents, knife-wielding hitchhikers and gun-toting ex-wives. By mutual agreement, an aging Maria was no longer cleaning or cooking for them, which meant the new mistress of the manse better get her ass in gear and figure it out. After a tour of the house, she sipped a mug of coffee and started a list.

Laundry, supermarket…

The unexpected chime of the doorbell made her hand twitch, sloshing coffee down the front of her last clean t-shirt. Perfect.

Every hair in place and dressed to the nines, Alyssa Prescott-Malone flashed a Beauty Queen smile. "You must be that little Shelton gal Jace keeps going on about. Aren't you the cutest thing? Is he here?"

For the second day in a row, she'd opened the door to a nightmare. What were the odds? "He's on his way to Austin to sort out some problems with a case."

"What case is that?"

"The man who raped and murdered his daughters."

"Honey, that case is a slam-dunk. I'm second-chair and I can assure you there are no problems. Knowing Jace, he made up that story to get a few days away from here, no offense. Oh, hell, I never could lie worth a damn. He asked me to come."

And for the second day in a row, the ground opened to swallow her whole. "I don't believe you."

Alyssa made a sympathetic pout with her lips. "Now look what I've done. I've upset you and I'm sorry. He said you were a little fragile because of your granddaddy's passing and all."

"You know about my grandfather?"

"Of course I do, honey. Jace told me all about you, how you lost your folks when you were a baby, your career, everything. Thanks for helping him, by the way."

"Helping him?"

"With his new book. Have you read it?"

The blood froze in her veins as she wrapped her arms around herself and shook her head. "He didn't want me to read it until he was finished."

"But you know what it's about, right? I swear that man is like a literary serial killer with his trophies and all."

"Trophies?" She hated this, the half-truths and lies, but what she truly despised were the seeds of doubt taking root.

"His little strays. When we were married, he'd go off for weeks, find some little gal with a story and indulge his kinks. Six months later, they'd wind up as the sympathetic waif in his latest book."

"Jace would never use me like that."

"Honey, writers live by a different set of rules. What we think of as exploitation, they consider research." Several sheets of paper appeared out of thin air, as if the witch had conjured them. "I was hoping I wouldn't have to show you these."

Her hand trembled as she took them. Emails. Emails regarding Sabrina Shelton. Emails requesting information about an incident in Afghanistan.

She didn't recognize the name of the recipient, but the sender was all too familiar. The facts were there, the lurid details. Skimming the dates, her eyes blurred. He'd sent the first one 5/21/2015 12:42:17 P.M. US Central Standard Time, an hour before he came for her at Gus's. She knew the date well. What woman would forget the day and hour the man of her dreams carried her off into the sunset?

*I'm a human being, not a storyline.* She remembered the exact moment she said that to him too. Three short weeks ago, they were in his kitchen and he was tending her knee. Had she suspected? Maybe. Probably. It didn't matter now. In the end, that's all she was, a storyline, fodder for his fiction, a *sympathetic waif* with benefits.

She thrust the emails back. "You've made your point. Is that all?"

"You keep 'em, honey. He also wanted me to give you this. It's a first-class ticket to Boston from San Antonio. He didn't want you driving all the way to Austin. The flight leaves at three o'clock today. I'm sure you don't want to hang around here. That'd be awkward, don't you think? I'll be seeing him later. Is there anything you want me to tell him?"

The madness wasn't behind them after all. For her, it was just beginning. Taking the envelope, she kept her tears at bay, and in a surprisingly strong voice, closed another chapter in her life. "Tell him I said good-bye."

# Chapter 33

"God's country needs a few more cell phone towers," Jace muttered, pocketing his cell phone. He'd been driving almost an hour without service. The hour or so before that, he'd tried at least a dozen times to reach Sabrina but all his calls went straight to voicemail.

He didn't like being out of touch, especially today. More for his peace of mind than hers, he wanted to hear her voice. Like everything else about her, he loved her voice. A tad on the low side, it was a little bit country, a little bit eastern sophisticate and a whole lot of sexy.

She'd handled the events of the morning like a champ, better than him. More of a 'take a breath and think things through' kind of guy, he wasn't one to go off half-cocked, except where that case concerned. Alyssa knew it too. She wasn't the brightest bulb in the pack, but she was smart enough to deduce he'd never forgive himself if the bastard walked free because he or Mike screwed the pooch.

He knew in his gut they'd done things by the book, and now that he'd had time to think about her phone call, things weren't adding up. From the very beginning, the defense had filed motion after motion to delay the trial in hope of getting a more sympathetic jury, so why the rush? There were other inconsistencies too, ones he hadn't bothered to look at until now. Mike lost his baby sister in a boating accident and hated the ocean, so why would he spend two weeks in the middle of it cooped up in a tiny stateroom? He wouldn't. Alyssa lied. The question was why.

Jerked from his thoughts, he reached for his cell phone. It wasn't Sabrina but he was relieved to have service again. It was Clay, and judging from the display, he'd left two prior voicemails. "You bored or just missing my pretty face?"

"Good thing you finally picked up. I was ready to come out there with a couple of crime scene investigators."

"You worry too much. Sabrina and I kissed and made up."

"Good to hear but…where are you?"

"About half an hour out of Austin. I have to deal with some issues on a case."

"Your ex wouldn't be involved in those issues, would she?"

He winced, his stomach dropping to the floorboard. "Why?"

"She breezed through town a couple of hours ago and made a stop at the café for directions to your place. I found out about it when I went over to grab some lunch, and I've been trying to get you on the phone ever since. Something didn't feel right."

"Sonofabitch!"

"Friend, you lead an interesting life. What can I do?"

"Put the CSIs on hold. If she's still there when I get back, I'm going to kill her."

The return trip was the longest two hours of his life. Thankfully, he didn't see her red Mercedes or he might have run it off the road. All he saw was the blur of the landscape and his own stupidity. What he refused to see was a life without Sabrina.

Any hope the women had missed one another was dashed when he got home and found the emails on the kitchen table. He had his laptop with him so there was no way Sabrina could have pulled them up and printed them. There was no way she'd stick around and wait for an explanation either, not his woman. She'd run—and this time he wouldn't blame her.

He found her at Gus's. Busy loading the Jeep with suitcases and boxes, she didn't miss a beat as he braked to a stop and flung open the door. "Sabrina, honey, we need to talk."

"So talk but make it quick. I'm on a schedule." She didn't turn around, just kept her back to him and went on stuffing things willy-nilly in the Jeep.

"I know Alyssa was at the house. What did she say to you?"

It was too little too late. He read it in the rigid set of her shoulders, the defiant lift of her chin when she whirled to confront him. "It's not important what she said. Are you going to stand there or are you going to help me with this stuff?"

He wanted flashing blue eyes and red cheeks, tears and pouty pink lips, but this wasn't the wild child who'd railed at him across a lonely country road. This was a woman who'd been to hell and back and wanted out, a woman who held his soul in the palm of her hand and whose destiny didn't include him.

"Alyssa means nothing to me. She never did."

Leaning a hip against the tailgate, she folded her arms beneath her breasts. "Is that why you practically pole-vaulted out of bed this morning? Seriously, Jace? The Ride of the Valkyries? Did you really think I wouldn't figure out whose ringtone that was? Among the myriad things you don't know about me is that I'm a sucker for Norse mythology. Valkyrie means 'chooser of the slain'. I'll ask you again. How damn dumb do you think I am?"

"Baby, you're not the dumb one here. Alyssa lied about the case going south to get me out of town. If Clay hadn't called and told me the bitch was nosing around at the café, I'd probably still have my head up my ass. I should have told you it was her this morning, but I didn't want to upset you."

"That worked out well, didn't it? Did she also lie about the emails because I'm pretty sure those were real?"

At this point, he had nothing to lose but his mind. "I sent them. I sent out about a dozen of them. I don't know how Alyssa got them and I don't care, and it doesn't matter how I found out. Knowing someone hurt you and got away with it tore me up. You might have died."

Hips swaying, head held high, she strolled toward him, another image imprinting on his brain. If she was determined to leave, at least he'd have that. Her hand came up to graze his cheek, a touch so soft he might have imagined it if it weren't for what he hoped he saw reflected in her eyes. "But I didn't die, and you need to let it go. I know Carly blabbed about Afghanistan. After Beauty Queen Barbie left and I had my third nervous breakdown for the week, I put the pieces together. Now will you please help me get this stuff in the Jeep? I'm running late."

"If you think I'm helping you leave me, you're nuttier than she is."

The air around him crackled as she dropped her jaw and threw her hands up in the air. "I'm not leaving you, dumbass. I'm donating this stuff and I have exactly twenty-five minutes before the collection place closes. And yeah, I know I'm going to be spanked for the dumbass remark but…"

His mouth claimed hers in a kiss that made the earth beneath them quake and the stars above collide. Relief and love surged through him as their passion came together in a dance as old as time. Sipping her sweetness, his tongue explored every ridge and hollow while his hands roamed her body, each dip and curve responding to his touch.

When it was over, she rested her cheek on his chest. "I'm not selling this place. The nearest safe house for battered women is in Middleton, an hour away, even longer for some of the towns south of us. I called Helen Davidson and offered her a ninety-nine year lease on the property. All she has to do is pay the utilities and taxes. She jumped at the chance to live here and run it." Her arms still wrapped around him, she glanced back at the house. "You think granddad would approve of the Augustus Shelton Safe Haven for Women?"

He'd been moved to tears three times in his adult life, when he buried his folks and Gus, but this wasn't about death. This was about life and love and compassion, the likes of which humbled him. "Baby, if I know Gus, he's up there busting with pride. You did all this in five hours?"

"You snooze, you lose, cowboy. That'll teach you to run out on me."

"What am I going to do with you?"

"You're going to marry me. Texas has a three-day waiting period but New Mexico doesn't, so if we leave tomorrow morning, we can be there by nightfall and get married on Monday."

He was laughing so hard he thought his ribs would crack. "I think that's a fine idea. Where are we heading for, Albuquerque, Santa Fe?"

"Roswell."

"Roswell as in weather balloons?"

"Roswell as in UFOs and get that smirk off your face. 'Condemnation without evidence is the height of ignorance.' Einstein said that and I couldn't agree more."

Refusing to let her go for even a second, he tightened his arms around her. "How many quotations have you memorized?"

"Enough to win every argument for the next fifty years. After that, I'll make them up as I go along."

# Chapter 34

"So how 'bout those UFOs?"

Bri rolled her eyes. "Explain something, Malone. How can someone who loves science fiction be so…"

"Smart, savvy, sane?"

"I was going to say poopy."

He gave her one of his devilish, pussy-melting grins. "I think my bride's a little cranky. We'll be home in forty-five minutes. Why don't you recline the seat and grab a nap."

Sleep was the last thing she wanted. Since the wedding, she'd developed an irrational fear of waking up to find she'd only dreamed the last four days.

She glanced down at her wedding ring, a plain gold band with Celtic knots encircling it, the one she wanted and almost didn't get. He'd been fixated on dropping a bundle for some platinum thing with pavé diamonds, whatever they were. It was beautiful but it wasn't her. When reason didn't work, she'd had to drag him out of the jewelry store to have a private word. There, in full view of a sales clerk hoping Daddy

Warbucks would dump Little Orphan Annie and come back with a girlie-girl, she fisted her hands on her hips.

*"Hello, have we met? I ride motorcycles. I like to go camping in inclement weather. I prefer Levis to Dolce and Gabbana, and I've never paid more than fifty dollars for a pair of shoes in my life. I don't need platinum and diamonds to prove how much you love me."* Pouting, she pulled off a sniffle or two. *"Besides, I want us to have matching bands."*

*"Are you playing me, brat?"*

*"Is it working?"*

*"Yep."*

Score! An hour later, they exchanged plain gold bands with Celtic knots in front of a Justice of the Peace. In a surprise move, she slipped the word *obey* into her vows and managed not to choke on it. There wasn't a snowball's chance in hell she'd always do it but sometimes a girl had to make a few concessions for the man of her dreams.

Drumming his fingers on the steering wheel, Jace peered in her direction. "I've been thinking about something. Now that we're married, maybe I should introduce you to maintenance spankings."

*Oh, hell.* She was preparing to rip off a saucy rejoinder when her cell phone beeped an incoming text message. "Saved by the bell." She read the message and saw her hope for a quiet evening go down the tubes. "It's Helen. She moved in yesterday and there's a problem with the water heater. The basement's flooded. What should we do?"

"Tell her we're on our way."

Forty minutes later, Bri rolled down her window and gawked. Aside from Tiny's on a Saturday night or church on Sunday morning, she'd never seen this many vehicles in the same spot at the same time in Serenity. Gus's private road was bumper-to-bumper, the overflow extending down the main road. "You don't suppose the house blew up, do you?"

"Not unless the Fire Department brought their own music and food. I smell barbecue."

Hand in hand, they walked toward the melee. She was still reeling from the throng of familiar faces and party atmosphere when someone fired a gun. A hush fell over the crowd as Clay climbed a makeshift dais. "In keeping with a tradition started almost twenty-five years ago by none other than Augustus Shelton himself, I'd like to introduce you all to a whole new generation of Malones, my best friend and his beautiful bride."

Amid the thunder of applause and whistles, a banner dropped from the eaves of the porch. *CONGRATULATIONS SABRINA AND JACE.*

Jace drew her close and brushed a kiss atop her head. "Doesn't look like there's going to be a mass exodus from Serenity anytime soon. Welcome home, Mrs. Malone."

She'd had enough bad days to appreciate the magical ones. There were three that came to mind, the day he claimed her, the day he married her and now this. It was hard to take it all in, the food, the musicians, the endless sea of smiles. Forgiveness and acceptance. Home.

Pushing his way through the well-wishers, Clay grabbed her by the shoulders. "Your husband can kick my ass later but I'm kissing the bride." A cheer went up as he planted a long, wet one on her lips.

Laughing hysterically, she feigned a swoon. "Wow. We need to find you a wife. It's a shame to let that go to waste. You did all this on your own?"

"Helen helped but Carly organized it. She didn't want to put a damper on things so she's hiding out inside the house. This is your day, honey, and no one's going to blame you if you're not ready."

Was she ready? It seemed petty to carry a grudge. More sister than friend, Carly had gone to a lot of trouble to mend the rift. Still, the betrayal cut deep, especially since she'd leveled her venom at Jace. She needed time to decompress and think about what to say to her, how to make her understand.

A gnarled hand touched her arm. "Sabrina?"

Startled, she spun around and stammered out a greeting. "Mrs. Fields. Thank you for coming."

"I wish you well, but I'm not here for the party. I need to talk to you."

"Is your husband here?"

"My husband wouldn't come." With surprising strength, the frail woman led her away from the group assembled near the dais. It was only when they were out of earshot that she loosened her grip. "I need to say my piece and then I'm going home."

From the corner of her eye, Bri saw Jace advancing on them. She'd seen that look before and it didn't bode well. She gave a small shake of her head and he backed off, but in those fleeting few seconds, she felt his love like a caress. He was there for her and always would be. She was basking in the glow of that amazing revelation when Mrs. Fields metaphorically smacked her upside the head.

"Is it true you gave Gus's house away?"

Memory of the ambush at the bar got her back up. "Yes, I did. Is that a problem?"

"Some kind of shelter for damaged women I hear."

"They're abused, Mrs. Fields. Not damaged."

"I want to help out, maybe cook or clean or something."

It was official. She'd wandered into *The Twilight Zone.* "Excuse me?"

"I want to volunteer. Am I too old?"

"Of course you're not too old. I'm sure someone with your maturity and wisdom will always be welcome. The pretty lady in blue talking to Doc Coleman is Helen Davidson, the Director. Go on over and introduce yourself. Tell her I sent you."

The older woman took her hand. "You're a good girl, Sabrina, but bitterness is a hard pill to swallow. That night at Tiny's, we saw the resemblance right off. You reminded us of our granddaughter. That's why my husband was hard on you."

"I don't understand."

"Our daughter did the best she could with her, but Janie was a wild one. She ran off with the first boy who came along with a car fast enough to get her away from here. He beat her. He beat her bad but he didn't kill her. She did that herself. She left a note sayin' no one cared enough to help her and she had nowhere to go. Maybe if she had someplace like this, she'd still be…you're doin' a good thing. Gus'd be proud."

"I hope so. I'm truly sorry about your granddaughter, Mrs. Fields. I didn't know."

"No one in Serenity knows, not even our pastor. We're proud people, Sabrina."

"You have my word, ma'am. I won't tell anyone."

"You just be happy, honey. A new beginning is as good a time as any to bury old sorrows. I'll go meet Miz Davidson and then I'll be off."

Bri watched the interaction between the two women. Worlds apart, so vastly different but with a singular goal, they smiled and chatted and eventually embraced.

*A new beginning is as good a time as any to bury old sorrows.* Damned if it wasn't. She found Carly in the kitchen. Up to her elbows in frosting, she was totally engrossed in putting the final touches on a Texas-size wedding cake. "Great party. Nice cake too, but if the topper is a man spanking a woman, you're in deep shit."

Carly didn't bat an eye or lift her head. "I couldn't find one. I even went online. You people need to organize and market yourselves better. I'm thinking coffee mugs and t-shirts."

"I'm thinking you should quit while you're ahead." *No one cared enough to help her and she had nowhere to go.* "I hate what you did but I love that you cared enough about me to make the effort."

"Bri, I was so wrong about everything, especially the way I went about it. You were right about me, but I'm trying, I really am. I did some research and talked to Helen about, you know."

"Domestic Discipline, Carly. It's okay to say out loud. Well, maybe not too loud."

"How can you joke about it? I almost ruined a lifelong friendship by being so…me."

"I'll admit I was angry and hurt, but I just learned there are worse things than having your best friend worry about your well-being. I'll say the same thing to you I said to Jace about Afghanistan, which by the way we'll discuss at another time, you need to let it go."

"Sabrina Ann Malone, you get your cute butt out here and dance with your husband."

Bri whirled in place, the disembodied voice tinny and mechanical—and loud. "What the hell was that?"

Grinning, Carly took off her apron. "That was Jace with a couple of beers under his belt and Tommy's megaphone from soccer practice. We'd better get out there before our husbands and my brother turn this into a frat party."

More people were arriving as they stepped out to the porch. Carly stopped her with a tug. "Look at them all. They're here for you, Bri, you and Jace. Level with me. That day in the café when I pointed him out to you, did it ever occur to you that you might end up with him?"

Transported back, Bri closed her eyes. *Well over six-feet with skin like burnished copper, he had a body beyond drool-worthy, muscled and toned, but it was his face that made her heart race. Framed by raven black hair that kissed his shoulders, it was chiseled and intense, a warrior's face.* What she didn't know then was the beauty of his spirit or the depth of his heart. Friend, lover, husband, he was all that and more.

Magically, when she opened her eyes, he was at the bottom of the steps, his hand extended to her. "Come on, darlin'. They're playing our song."

As she was whirled off the porch toward the dance floor, she looked back at Carly and blew a kiss. "Hell yes, I knew. Some things were just meant to be."

# Books by
# Shelby Kent-Stewart

## *Erotic Romance*

Surviving Sydney
Blessing
Runaway Brat
Once Upon a Faerie
Storming Jericho

## *Thriller*

A Prudent Man

## *Humor*

Whiskered Words of Frisky Felines

# AUTHOR'S NOTE

Domestic violence in the US has reached epidemic proportions with close to one-third of American women reporting physical or sexual abuse by a husband or boyfriend at some point in their lives. In households with children where domestic violence occurs, the children are abused 60 percent of the time.

There are ways we can help. If you know someone at risk, find a way to let her know help is out there or report the abuse. Since most women suffering at the hands of a violent spouse or partner arrive at shelters and safe houses with nothing more than their children in tow and the clothes on their backs, donations of money and clothing are gratefully accepted. We're in this together.

**U.S. Hotline: 800-799.SAFE (7233)**
**Teen Dating Abuse Hotline: 866.331.9474**

Peace, Shelby

# ABOUT THE AUTHOR

A native of Southern California, Shelby is no stranger to the wonderful world of words. With the publication of her first short story at the ripe old age of ten, she was hooked. Since then, she has enjoyed careers as a political speech writer, an advertising copywriter and an author of mainstream fiction with occasional forays into erotic romance. "The world is cold. Romance and great sex heat it up."